The Amok Runners

By Colin Cotterill

D0465231

The Amok Runners
Copyright © Colin Cotterill, 2016
First Published 2016

This edition published by
DCO Books
Proglen Trading Co., Ltd.
Bangkok Thailand
http://www.dco.co.th

ISBN 978-1533265289

In loving memory of Khin Than Aye, wife of Clive.

Also by Colin Cotterill

Dr. Siri Paiboun series

Jimm Juree series

Other publications

Contents

Prologue

"Murdered. And somebody's responsible."
Plan Nine From Outer Space. (1959)

Sergeant Chat had ridden to the crime scene on his personal Honda Dream. It had a Serpico sticker on the back mud flap. The afternoon was 38 degrees centigrade but he wore a white Siam Commercial Bank windcheater over his uniform shirt. As soon as he stepped off the bike, beads of sweat formed on his forehead like wax melting off a deep-orange temple candle. The pomelo grove workers had discovered the body floating in the pond and now they stood staring as if they expected it to flip onto its back and do tricks. Chat told them they could go back to their work. This was police business. When they didn't respond he raised his voice, 'Go!' They shrugged and shuffled off till they were swallowed by the tree line.

Once he was alone, Chat shook his head and unbuckled his belt. For a Thai police officer nothing was straightforward. You were paid barely enough to live, you got no respect, and you were still expected to take care of bodies – alive or otherwise. He pulled off his boots and removed his trousers, folding them neatly over a branch. He'd only had his new uniform a week. The water was luminous green and it stank. He hung his shirt over the 'Chemicals, No Swimming' sign. He looked around for a heavy hunk of wood but fortune favoured him with a slab of concrete two feet long. He was a twig of a policeman and at first he could barely lift it but he managed to claw it free of the weeds and cradle it out into the water. With each step he sank

1

deeper into the mud. Whatever chemicals were dumped there hadn't completely decimated the pond life which in some ways was a good thing. But there was movement around his legs and beneath his feet. He hoped it was fish and not the Naga spirit of the water about to pull him down into its depths. And pray to the Lord Buddha - not snakes. He could abide snakes even less than demons.

The pond was more of a saucer than a bowl. When he arrived at the unclothed body, the water barely reached his briefs. He could see the bullet hole through the woman's scalp. The wound was clean and busy with flies. But that's all he bothered to take in. He had no intention of spending more time with her than necessary. He thanked his stars that she was a broad woman with plenty of back. With his arms trembling he let out a puff of air and rested the concrete along her spine. She sank, not like a stone, more like a crippled oil tanker. She listed first this way then the other before disappearing beneath the surface. He held onto the slab until the body was securely pinned to the mud.

Chat looked around once more to check the rim of the pomelo groves and a distant deserted road. Certain his shifty work had been undetected, he trudged back to the bank. As he dressed he kept his eye on the smooth greasy surface of the pond. His job was done. Now it was up to the algae and the water pollution to do theirs.

Prologue 2

"... you've got to ask yourself a question: Do I feel lucky?"
Dirty Harry (1971)

Dear Clint,

That was what you movie people might call a 'teaser'. As the daughter of a fisherman I'd prefer to call it a lure and I know for certain you've got the hook in your cheek now.

But first, the niceties.

I hope this email finds you in a better frame of mind. I'd like to think you had little input into the silly threatening PDF we received from your lawyer last month. I'm certain she and you realize that a restraining order only applies to our physical presence in your life, and not, as yet, to stalking by internet (SBI). As you are in California and my sister-cum-brother, Sissy, and I are all the way over here in Thailand, there is little chance of us climbing over your garden wall and stealing underwear from your clothesline. (Unless you decide to send us air tickets – ha ha). And as the world cyber policing community has yet to commit to a legal definition of 'hacking' as opposed to accidentally stumbling into an office computer network, you must realize that there is no legal way to be rid of us.

To be fair, we are hardly your enemy, dear Clint. You must admit that Sissy's recommendations on how to protect your budgeting software have led to a much safer security system for Malpasa Films, even though she can still access them. Once you sit back with a glass of beer and look at our relationship objectively, you'll realize what a potential gold mine it could be. Don't forget we could take all our scenarios and scripts to other companies. Don't worry, we would never do that. We have loved you as both a cowboy and a director for most of our lives and we

3

are determined to have you as our launching pad into the stratosphere of cinematic entertainment.

But first some sad news. Perhaps you saw on CNN about the devastating tidal surge in December that took chunks out of the coastline along the Gulf of Thailand. As a result, the Lovely View Resort and Restaurant (which I'm sure you have come to see as a friend featuring in our two most recent screenplay offerings) was washed completely out to sea. Our home is no more. The land in which our deranged mother, Mair, invested her entire life savings now lies at the bottom of the gulf. Consequently, my family is destitute and scattered. Mair has moved into the cabin of Captain Kow, our long-lost father. My bodybuilder brother, Arny, is shacking up with his elderly fiancé. Ex traffic cop, grandfather Ja, has moved south to set up a detective agency with an old colleague, and I am back home in Chiang Mai in Sissy's spare room.

But I don't want to bore you too much with our domestic strife, nor make you feel that our pleas for recognition have become desperate. In fact, the purpose of this email is to pass on good news. Out of every pile of buffalo dung a pretty toadstool grows. As you know I am a journalist at heart, if not currently in practice. But in my heydays I was the hottest crime reporter at the Chiang Mai Mail. Sissy and I were recently recalling some of my greatest hits over a bottle of Chilean red. And the story we recalled with the greatest affection was 'The Case of the Amok Runners'.

Clint, really, it has everything; murder, Hollywood stars, sex, corruption and the best damned treasure hunt I've ever been involved in. As I have plenty of time on my hands at the moment I decided to knock it into shape for your consideration. Trust me, this is the one. I would have gone ahead and written it as a screenplay but I know how touchy you are about such things. I *tell you, hang onto your Stetson, Clint baby, because this story throws all our other submissions into the dark shadows.*

Mr. E, we know that you have reluctantly become a team player in the massive corporate game but inside you are still just like us. Admit it, you admire our passion. Before Wagon Train, you had dreams like ours. You wanted to make a difference. Dirty Harry, the man with no name and the orangutan guy all had to fight the suits to stick to their principles. It was only through perseverance that you made it to the top of the hill. Without great people like you and little but emerging talents like us there would be no art, no independent cinema and no passion.

So, Clint, sit back and revel in the delights of your next blockbuster.

Your greatest admirers,
Jimm and Sissy
(Address withheld)

Chapter 1

"It's such a fine line between stupid and clever."
This Is Spinal Tap (1984)

We were on the veranda, stoned. We had a darkening blurry view of most of Chiang Mai; me, Sissy, brother Arny and an unconscious Burmese called Khin.

'Four,' said Sissy.

'Four, what?' I asked.

'That's when I knew I was in the wrong body,' he said. 'That was the turning point.'

'What of?'

'Of my life, Girl. Come on. Pay attention! You asked me a question. You've gotta stay focused long enough to get an answer.'

There was no reason on earth why we should have been yelling at each other in English let alone with New York accents. We're Thai, and apart from a disastrous home-stay in Melbourne I'd hardly spent any time out of the country. It was all Mair's fault. Our mother had wanted us to be children of the world so she'd only spoken to us in Thai at weekends. For most of our lives we thought she was foreign. We picked up the accents from movies. We became bilingual and disjointed simultaneously.

'You became a girl when you was four?' I asked.

When you were being New Yorkers you were supposed to say 'fuck' a lot but I wasn't that partial to it.

'Yeah.'

'Nobody changes gender when they're four, brother. At four you don't even know the rules yet.'

'I did.'

'You're messed up.'

Sissy took another toke and held in the smoke, giving himself a stupid tight-lipped smile. He was wearing one of my sun dresses. On me it looked like drapery. On Sissy it was a figure-hugging shroud. I'd stopped growing vertically at twelve but continued to expand horizontally. It wasn't fair that he had the body I'd fantasized for myself. This would be his last night as a woman for a while. The next morning he'd be strapping his chest and walking with a swagger.

We had a mountain between us and the setting sun but in the distance the windows of the Ping River condominiums reflected its pink. There was a dirty orange tint to the sky. I was always impressed by the stains smeared across the Chiang Mai scenery by the March crop burn-offs. It would have made a good picture if I'd had a telephoto lens - if I'd seen any point in owning a camera. They were already making cell phones that took pictures but I'd have preferred a camera that talked to you; told you what you were doing wrong.

'It's true,' Sissy said. 'Four's the turning point. You make a bad call. It sets you off on the wrong track and next thing you know you're in a corrections facility mopping floors.'

Sissy was never in jail. He'd become nominally female when he was in his teens and had a good life in transvestite cabarets, progressing to transsexual media entertainment, gender realignment and marriage – to a man. He looked at me. His expression was as flat as a paddy after a monsoon. The dope was sending him into a funk. It made me laugh through my nose and launch off on a giggle fit but he sat paddy-faced and solemn.

'Let's see if Khin thinks my early slide into transexualism is a laughing matter,' he said. 'Khin!'

We looked to the shape in the third seat.

Silence.

'Obviously not.'

'She's dead, man,' I said.

Khin's head hung over the back of the recliner with her mouth open like a fat-lipped ceremonial trumpet. The Burmese was built like a pipe. All those life-giving fluids and gasses had to pass up and down that narrow drain of a woman so it wasn't surprising a few puffs of ganja might overpower her. Two cans of beer had the same effect. She never could keep up with me and Sissy. We watched her gasp for air. In six hours she'd be bloodied up and thrown into turmoil for fifteen hundred baht a day – not an insignificant sum for an illegal Burmese.

Beyond Khin, in the last seat sat my younger brother, Arny, a magnificent specimen of musculature erected at the Body Great Gymnasium over fifteen years. He spoke little and despite the fact that he looked like a professional wrestler he was a pussy cat. He wasn't asleep but he might as well have been. We often forgot he was there.

Not for the first time, we languished peacefully on white plastic sun beds stolen from the pool of the Rincome Hotel. We were the odd foursome – the first line of a joke. 'A fat girl, a bodybuilder, a transsexual and a Burmese historian were sitting on a deck overlooking the shimmering night lights of Chiang Mai.

The fat girl turned to the transsexual and said, 'What are we again?'

'No shortage of answers to that, sister,' said Sissy.

'I mean tomorrow.'

'We're amok runners,' he said.

'Right. Right. And what is that again?'

'We're the guys that panic.'

'So 'amok' …?'

'Means panic. Kind of.'

'So, I can say, "Okay guys, don't amok!".'

'I knew you'd find a way of screwing that up. No, you can't.'

'Why not?'

'If you don't use it with 'run', nobody'll know what you're talking about.'

'Got it.'

I didn't get it. Sissy had left my English in his dust when he got hooked up with the internet. He'd learned pretty much everything apart from how to hang on to a partner and keep the looks that had won him beauty titles in his twenties. He was forty now and starting to look used up. That's why he only ventured out at night. He'd retreat to his room and was attempting to set up a fruitful business empire on-line. He only ever emerged to make movies and for that he disguised himself as a man. I had to call him, 'he'. It was hard.

'And, what are we run amoking from?' I pushed.

'I'd have to assume we're run amoking from each other,' Sissy decided. '*Amok* suggests a lack of teamwork. He pointed to the ground where documents had been fanned across the veranda by an evening breeze. They lay like stepping stones all the way to the sheer drop. According to these here extras notes, we're all pretty much chasing around like headless chickens for a few days.'

'Do we get to die?' I asked.

'Repeatedly, I'd say. It's kind of a reusable reincarnation. They sent me to Nirvana six times in Alexander. They just give you a fresh uniform with a brand new mortal wound and send you off to die another death.'

'Cool.'

'It's a blast.'

Sissy had almost been a television starlet in his pretty days. Channel Three had put together a drama around him but he couldn't act. People tuned into the first few programs because of the novelty of it all. He was the first transvestite – non slapstick clown - female lead on television. (This was before the snip.) Once they realized he had no talent they deserted him. He had one or two moments in advertisements but never made it back to prime time. So, whenever there was a foreign movie shot in Thailand he'd apply to be an extra. He pumped up the macho when he was on set. He still hoped he'd be discovered and pulled from the ranks of amok runners. It never happened.

The conversation staggered through other topics but inevitably fell back into the arms of the movie profession.

'I got a question, Sissy,' I said.

'They call me Wikipedia.'

'Why is Dan Jensen starring in this movie?'

'Because he's hot.'

'I know that, but what I mean is; historically, what justification is there for his presence? Him getting wounded in ancient Greece or Vietnam I can understand ... but what are his firm white buttocks doing here in Thailand in the sixteenth century getting tortured by the Burmese?'

'Exactly.'

'You're such a racist.'

'It ain't racist, brother. He couldn't have been here.'

'Yes, he could. And do you know how I know he could?'

'Tell me.'

The joint was bite-sized now. Sissy pulled his famous roach clip from his handbag and nipped the remains.

'Because ... and it's really important you take notes on this one ... because if there weren't any white guys here it'd erase some five hundred million dollars in box office revenue in mainland USA alone. Nobody wants to see a bunch of ethnics massacring each other without American help. If he wasn't here there'd be no marketable reason for making the movie. By shipping in Dan – ooh look at my teeth everyone – Jensen and having him master eight words of Thai with which to turn the depleted Siamese army into a fit, hungry fighting force, they've upped the budget a zillion times. So, if America says it was here in 1560 ...'

'But there wasn't even an America in 1560.'

'What's a hundred years give or take to your average cinema-goer?'

'Oh, man,' I said. 'It's my history.'

'And, if you ask me, it needs serious editing. Who cares? We're talking fiction here. You'll be telling me next *The King and I* got it wrong.'

'Don't get me started on that.'

'It's backdrop. Get over it. Either that or withdraw in protest. Handcuff yourself to the Three Kings monument downtown and go on a fast and tell the world the Americans are doing a re-write on our heritage.'

'Then I wouldn't get to be in a movie.'

'That's the spirit exactly. We have to get those priorities straight. You're almost a star. Forty-six dollars a day plus meals; can't sniff at that.'

This was going to be my first *extra* role but I wasn't doing it for the money. I'd been given the go ahead from the editor to do a series of reports from the front line. But once I signaled my intention it turned into a family affair. Our brother, Arny had signed up, and, to my dismay, Mair insisted on coming along too. Cinematic bonding, she called it. It was just as well they were recruiting 'Assorted Asians' for the early scenes. We were more assorted than most. Only Grandad Ja, grumpy as ever, was staying home to run the family shop. Sissy and I remained philosophical about it all. How many families had a Hollywood home movie to show their great grand children?

'You're right,' I said.

Chiang Rai ganja taught you to observe. You'd notice things. That's why I liked it. The lights of the municipal grid had replaced the lights of heaven. Headlights and taillights danced a slow polonaise along Huay Gaew Road. Advertising hoardings dazzled brazenly beside the super highway. The city spread before us like a buffet of shiny rhinestones.

In fact, Thailand itself was more bluster than salience those days. There had been times when military coups landed on the country like raindrops. The population had become so inured to the seasonal sprinkles that Thais had long since stopped complaining. The common people took their ideological soakings without protest and left the rabble rousing to the students. A succession of military tsars helped themselves to the spoils of government and everyone applauded their chutzpa.

But in recent times there were longer gaps between the dark clouds and there had even been periods of dubious democracy. Then, three years earlier, a sun-god rose in the north and spread light and free gifts across the land. He dawned with such brilliance that all of the little political parties gelled into one under his banner. And he warmed the earth with his big smiling Chinese face. And he set, not on the cities, but on the villages for that was his vote base. He introduced cheap medical schemes and rural development projects and protection from the drug mafias for the poor and they bowed before him.

And all the while he dug his hand into the same coffers of power from which the famous coup generals before him had feathered their nests. His once obscene wealth became scandalous and soon he owned not only the position of Prime Minister but the country itself. And a great envy descended upon the land and the sleeping military was awoken and the sun-king was banished to a distant kingdom where he bought condominiums and football clubs and got blisters on his fingers from counting his ill-gotten off-shore funds. So it was we sat there beneath the cloud of yet another military administration.

It was at that moment that Khin spluttered out of her nightmare.

'Yes? What? What?'

'Welcome back, Khin,' I said. 'How was the trip?'

'I thought, I … I thought I was in purgatory.'

'No, Khin,' Sissy reminded her. 'You left purgatory two years ago. You're in Thailand, now.'

'Thank heavens. What time is it?'

'Coming up to midnight.'

'Yes. My word. We have to run amok at the crack of dawn.'

Khin rose from the sun bed and unknotted her limbs like a newborn Bambi. She was unnecessarily tall, acne'd and eccentric. Her sensible hair and clothes always hung from her as if they were damp.

'You excited about it, Khin?' Sissy asked.

'Cock-a-hoop, my friend. Cock-a-hoop.'

She got to her feet, swayed a little, and headed off to the outside bathroom. I shook my head. Half the stuff she said I didn't recognize as English. She'd had a British education which tends to make people incomprehensible. I turned to Sissy.

'So, is she excited or what?'

'Very.'

'Why can't she just say so? She's got this whole language of her own. I don't hear other Brits talking like they've got Shakespeare stuck up their rear ends.'

'Ah, but don't forget, the British Isles changes with the times. It's open to international influences. Burma's been stuck in a time warp for the past forty years. Khin probably learned her English from Gilbert and Sullivan.'

I thought about it.

'They're old English guys, right?'

'Right.'

Chapter 2

**"I want you to drain every ounce of their blood,
even if it kills them."**
Teenage Mutant Ninja Turtles (2014)

'Siam' was the title of Hollywood's latest over-budget
goose. It was the week before the heavies arrived from
Los Angeles and two thousand other extras would be
added to the payroll for the big battle scenes.
Meanwhile they had to shoot the segments with
assorted Asians acting as village folk. We were under
the tutelage of local director, Pongpun Wichaiwong,
more intimately known as Boon. He'd brought his own
film crew from Bangkok and there were three Thai
television actors who, according to Sissy, were famous.
I didn't watch a lot of TV. They'd be the ones who got
to scream in close ups. An ex-Navy Seal stalwart had
flown in from the states to tutor us all in falling over
and throwing ourselves to the ground as if projected by
a bomb blast.

In all, we numbered a hundred; a good size to work
with. There were two scenes to be assembled; one, a
Burmese patrol being ambushed by half-a-dozen
American mercenaries and the other, a platoon running
amok after being sprayed by deadly liquid poison from
a fleet of paper hot-air balloons. As neither scene
involved name actors they'd been entrusted to Director
Boon. He had eighteen Thai films under his belt, three
of which had won awards at international festivals. For
'Siam', his name would appear deep down the credits
under 'in-country direction unit', but for these two
three-minute segments, he would make more than the

15

gross for his last four movies. Some might argue that this prostitution was below a respected cinematographer but Boon was a pragmatist and an artist. He rarely received the budgets he requested from Thai studios so this was a chance to spend rashly and show what he could do.

Quite apart from being a genius, Boon was also what Sissy would call, 'a lad'. His regular crew worshipped him and the extras working with him that week quickly joined the ranks of admirers. He'd brought everyone salted cashews from his small plantation in the south. He made play of work. He explained what he was doing and how he hoped to achieve it and he partied with the menials. He was a great general at ease with his troops.

On the Tuesday, Mair and Arny were off getting bloodied for an upcoming massacre. Sissy, Khin and I found ourselves eating lunch with Boon at the foot of Chiang Mai's own Grand Canyon. Deep in the southern suburbs across the Samoeng road were the remains of a fantastic project conceived during the building boom. Land owners leased out rights to dig for laterite and gravel. The greater the need, the deeper the open mines were sunk until the earth was pitted with gaping trenches. The deepest of these was some fifty yards down and two hundred yards across. The effect was spectacular. It had everything an ambush could ask for: towering but fragile cliffs, crevasses to hide in, and pretty water turned turquoise by the deep iron and aluminum deposits. The team had been shooting there since six in the morning and the caterers had delighted all but the most unadventurous foreigners by turning up with glutinous rice and fermented fish *lahp* for lunch. Many of the crew and extras were from the northeast so this was a treat.

'This was your idea.' Sissy didn't bother to make it a question for Boon. They'd first met when Boon was stage manager at a large transvestite cabaret in Pattaya then again on the TV soap. Like most people who'd met Sissy, he'd kept in touch. It was through him she got her extra work. The director broke off a nugget of sticky rice and dipped it in the fish sauce. He sat opposite us cross-legged on the ground with a broad, gibbon-like grin across his face.

'What makes you think that?' he asked.

He was fluent in symbolism and narrative but had little English so our group spoke in Thai. Khin was left behind. She could translate the most ancient Siamese texts and read temple inscriptions unfathomable to the average local but that left her trailing in live conversations by some four hundred years.

'Because you give a shit,' Sissy replied. 'I bet the great white bosses ordered sandwiches and you changed the order.'

'All that white bread takes the fight out of a man,' he said. 'Sticky rice leaves something burning in the heart.'

'Teacher,' I addressed the older man respectfully and bowed my head slightly, 'what are the Americans going to do when they discover your scenes are more beautiful and make theirs look like crap?'

Boon laughed from his gut. He was fifty with a paunch and he gathered up his long grey hair into a colourful scrunchie. He wore denim so weather-bleached and tight it looked like a layer of dry skin on him. His face was round and pinchable like a baby's, but with long straggly chin hair.

'Oh,' he smiled, 'no problem. They have software over there that can make anything look ordinary.'

He laughed again, scooped up a wad of rice and fish and fed it into his happy mouth. Even when eating he asked questions. He had an insatiable creative hunger and thirst for knowledge. After only ten minutes with our eclectic group he knew more about us than our own mothers which, in my case, I concede, wasn't that hard. He had filed away the fact that I was a journalist, single, probably unmarriageable and that Khin was a fanatical researcher.

'So,' he said, 'we'll have a real Burmese amid the legions of fake ones. Great.'

'She's a full-time international student at Chiang Mai University,' I lied. The fewer people who knew Khin was illegal the better.

'The three of you seem very close.'

'Closer than the three kings,' I announced proudly.

At the center of the moat city in the place of honour in front of the old City Hall was the monument to the three kings: Mangrai, Ramkamhaeng, and Ngammeuang. In 1296, King Mangrai, the local regent, invited the kings of Payao and Sukhothai to advise him on a proposed site for the new capital of the Lanna region soon to be called Chiang Mai. It was politicking at its most blatant but it ensured a lifetime union between the three. It was an alliance that had weathered a number of storms before it became a friendship but the three kings came to represent tolerance and common sense over the usual opportunism and butchery of the day.

'I'm Mangrai,' Sissy confirmed.

'Damn it,' I said. 'You always gets to be Mangrai.'

'Tell me it's a coincidence me and the great warrior were born on October 2nd,' said Sissy. 'I'm reincarnated, Boon. You're sitting before the great-to-the-power-of-something grandson of King Mangrai.'

'Not his queen?' asked Boon. Sissy ignored the comment.

'Great-granddaddy Mangrai was the man up here, Teacher Boon,' he said. 'He capitulated all the lands in the north, up into Burma and China, then through stealth and horrific violence he brought great peace upon the region. All the surrounding kingdoms looked up to him and admired his lack of morals. My sister, Jimm here is the King of Sukhothai because she thinks with her fanny. Her ancestor had an affair with the wife of the King of Phayao and got away with it. Khin's obviously the King of Phayao cause she's got no idea what's going on around her.'

'See, Teacher? We know it all,' I said, resenting the accusation that I thought with my fanny. 'If you need to hire us any time as historical advisors I guess we could arrive at a rate to make the three of us happy.'

Boon was enjoying the show.

'Well,' he said. 'I'm not sure I'd believe a word you two say, but I've got some projects coming up soon. I'm interested in your Burmese scholar, here. I bet she has a wealth of knowledge I could tap into.'

'I'm her agent,' I cut in.

'I do her hair and makeup,' Sissy added.

'We come as a set,' I said.

Khin was now only 371 years behind the conversation. When the translation caught up with her she reacted by telling us she didn't come cheaply. An exiled Burmese had to make a living where she could, but she insisted on working only one day out of three.

'She's got something else on?' Boon asked.

'Khin's even more distracted than usual these days,' Sissy told him. 'She's on a …'

'I don't think we need to trouble the director with the details of Khin's project,' I interrupted.

'She's on a treasure hunt,' said Sissy, ignoring me as usual.

I switched to English. 'Shut up, Bro!'

'What?'

'It's a secret.'

'This is Khin, man,' she said. 'It's not gonna take anyone long to notice she ain't a real normal lady.'

'Exactly. Do you think this man's going to hire Khin if he knows she's a nut ball?'

'Treasure?' Boon asked.

'Nah, I was just kidding,' said Sissy, switching back to Thai. 'She comes across a lot of weird shit in her research.'

'Treasure hunts are big in movies now,' said Boon. 'I could see a place for a Thai clue chase story. The *Da Vinci Code* and *National Treasure* grossed big. If she's got any ideas …'

'I don't know …' I said.

'I could, say, fund her research for a few more months and see if she comes up with something we could write a script from.'

I looked at Sissy who nodded.

'Well, there are a lot of interesting stories she's fond of telling us.'

'I'd like to hear some.'

I translated for Khin being careful to point out we hadn't given away any secrets.

'You can make something up,' I told her.

'Then I'm keen as mustard,' said Khin.

'Good,' I said and turned to Sissy. 'That means 'yes', right?'

'Sure does.'

'How did you all get together, if you don't mind my asking?' Boon said.

'We met in a bookshop,' Sissy told him. Boon's face expressed his doubt. 'No, serious. Me and Jimm used to hang out in one of the secondhand bookshops near the Thapae Gate. We found Khin in there one day.'

'Under *K*,' I added.

Khin had arrived in Chiang Mai from the University of Rangoon two years earlier. She'd come officially as a scholar and researcher to spend two months at the history department of Chiang Mai University. When her two months were up she'd refused to go back. She'd walked into the dean's office, sat in her uncomfortable visitor's chair and claimed academic asylum. She explained that the junta in her own country was suppressing academic freedom and stifling the rights of scholars to accurately document Burmese history.

It had been a difficult moment for CMU administrators. Khin Thein Aye was a respected historian and the scandal of having her arrested and deported would have lost the university a good deal of face in the international community. Face was practically all they had left so they dealt with the situation in the same way that many problems are solved in Southeast Asia. They pretended to know nothing about it. Officially, Khin had returned to Rangoon after her two-month tenure. They ceased to pay her per diem, removed her name from the list of visiting professors, and 'poof' the problem had vanished. They had no idea who this lanky woman stalking the history reading room and poring over palm leaf manuscripts might be.

Khin had become disconnected and broke simultaneously. It was a chance meeting with Sissy and me at a secondhand bookshop that prevented her from eating the palm leaf manuscripts she was working on. We'd scratched around to find her under-the-table English tutoring and translating work. For one brief period we even had her in uniform as a night watchman at a housing estate. I got her the rented house for next to nothing. On occasions she received small royalties for her articles in foreign publications. As she seemed to spend very little of her income and occupied much of her days agonizing over deadly serious texts, this humble income had kept her alive for two years.

Her parents had died of preventable diseases they couldn't afford to have treated. Her only brother had been shot in the student protests of 88, so Khin had nobody to send money to and no homesickness for a country she didn't like that much.

'We just sort of fell in love with her and made her our mascot,' I told Boon.

'That's very touching,' Boon smiled. 'What say we start tomorrow night? I'd like you three to come over to the hotel for drinks. Say eight?'

'Sounds good,' I said.

But for Khin's constant whining about 'irregularities', the afternoon ambush went comparatively smoothly.

'They're carrying flintlocks, Jimm. Flintlocks. Half a century before the things were conceived. Daft as brushes the lot of them.'

'Just keep limping, Khin, and shut up,' I said.

'A fine kettle of fish.'

'Relax, girl,' I said. 'Enjoy the show.'

Our mother had failed to make the cut for this scene due to the fact that she was annoying. She'd insisted on telling the acting director what to do. There was also the fact that Mair tended to be a bit dotty from time to time. Movie directors need people who follow orders and don't burst out laughing when hit by boiling oil. So we put her on a *songtaew* taxi and sent her home. That was the end of her movie career.

We remaining ambushees were all daubed in dark foundation that made us look like minstrels. The makeup lady had insisted on applying a layer to Khin. She told her she wasn't quite chocolate enough to pass for a Burmese. I hadn't bothered to translate. At the sound of a whistle we doomed stragglers dawdled through the manmade canyon. On the second whistle we looked anxiously to the heavens and scattered as imaginary rocks came raining down upon us. Earlier in the day, my brothers, Arny and Sissy and their fellow American counterparts (all English teachers at the American University Alumni Language Center) had rolled those same imaginary rocks off the cliff and fired their improbable weapons down into the valley below. At some much later stage in a studio, pixilated rocks would be married to the film and theatre audiences would go, 'ooh' and turn away as the digital brains of me and Khin squirted out of our crushed skulls.

The time wasn't so far off when they wouldn't need people to push the rocks or locations to push them into. The day would come when home viewers would select their favourite actor, do a right click and there he'd be embedded miraculously in a movie fashioned entirely on a computer. Then there'd be guest appearances. Doris from Oshkosh Wisconsin would find herself beneath the heaving muscular body of Vin Diesel, clawing her nails into his back. But, until that happened there was a need for Khin to throw herself on the ground several times and scream in Burmese. That scream would later be replaced by more convincing Burmese cries in a sound lab in Culver City; one more victim of the ever shrinking dominance of major Hollywood studios.

Chapter 3

"If you're good at something, never do it for free."
The Dark Knight (2008)

When we arrived at the Dhara Dhevi hotel, we weren't allowed to walk from the car park to reception. We were crammed into a hansom cab – Arny taking up two seats – pulled by some kind of stunted donkey to the front steps. This could be interpreted by some as 'class' but we thought it was ludicrous and chuckled the whole two minute journey. The pinkly shrouded receptionist phoned through to the room, spoke in hushed tones, and asked us if we wouldn't mind taking a seat for a few minutes. Director Boon had visitors.

A smiling girl brought us sugary bell fruit drinks for our inconvenience and we sat on stuffed seats in reception casting our eyes around that alien planet. It was what you got for anything up to six grand a night; a teakwood spa with your own yoga teacher, shoe shines, whirlpool baths, a working rice paddy with running coolies and abundant photo opportunities, antiques to smash in the comfort of your own room, ten foot ceilings, silk and marble and all the Thai smiles you could absorb in a lifetime. If that was how the other half lived you'd want to cross over to that other side as soon as you could.

Khin cringed in her seat.

'I think perhaps I should have worn another skirt,' she said.

'You don't have another skirt, Khin,' I reminded her.

'I certainly do.'

'Then why do you always wear that same long pink number?'

'Yes, in fact it's salmon, and I have three identical ones.'

Our laughter ruffled the neat atmosphere.

'Holy shit, Khin,' Sissy slapped her boney Burmese knee. 'You gotta be the only girl on the planet who owns three unfashionably long pink skirts. You're a one off.'

As this was an evening appointment and an occasion of sorts, Sissy was a woman for the night. He wore skin-tight leather pants, heels and a low-cut lavender blouse. His breasts had been let out for the evening. His hair was gelled upright and he'd spent a lot of time on his makeup. When he was a woman he wouldn't be seen dead without his face on. That was why he always played male extra parts rather than female. They'd never be able to smear mud on my brother as a sister. He was very sensitive as a she.

Khin, on the other hand, was a difficult woman to insult.

'They were the last three in stock at Mrs. Aye Than's needlework shop,' she said. 'They normally cost a pretty penny but she allowed me a discount as she had been acquainted with my mother. And I must point out, Jimm, you never seem to be complete without your somewhat too small T-shirts designed for a much younger person.'

Ooh, it hit.

'At least they're different colours,' I replied grumpily.

Arny thought that was hilarious.

Two short-haired Thai men in grey safari shirts and reinforced shoes strutted through reception on their way out. Sissy gave me a knowing glance. We were familiar with the type. The off-duty garb of men more comfortable in uniform. Private limousine drivers and school principals dressed like this hoping to carry the same menace but it rarely worked. Only men with stripes and ribbons in their closet could make casual wear look like a suit of armor. They'd just passed our seats when one turned around and glared at me. He seemed to know me although I had no idea who he was. I didn't realize at the time how significant that glare would prove to be.

After five minutes the reception telephone chirruped politely and the young lady had the bellboy escort us to Director Boon's suite. I noticed two things when Boon opened his door. Firstly, for a brief second, a different man stood before us – a nervous humorless version of the likeable hero. But as if Boon realized this too, he laughed and his old self stepped out through his skin. It all happened within a blink of an eye but I knew something disturbing had taken place to make him lose grip of his personality.

'Ah, my oddball friends,' Boon smiled. 'Come in. Come in.'

The second thing I noticed was that the director had his left hand hidden behind his back so he couldn't return our *wai*s. At first I imagined a gun there, or a gift, but when the Thai produced his hidden hand like a conjurer it was wrapped in a white napkin. One or two dots of blood had oozed to its surface.

'What happened?' Sissy asked.

'They call me Boon the accident prone,' the director laughed. 'I slipped in the bathroom, grabbed hold of the doorframe to steady myself, and the damn door slammed shut on me. Don't think it's broken. It only just happened so I haven't had chance to put anything on it.'

'Nor to think of a better story,' I mumbled in English. I stepped up to Boon and took hold of the hand. 'Can I take a look at it?'

'It'll be all right,' Boon said.

'You should let Jimm take a look,' Sissy told him. 'She used to be a brain surgeon.'

'I thought you were an investigative journalist,' said Boon.

'Yeah, the brain surgery was a weekend job,' I said. 'Red Cross, advanced course. Can I see?'

I removed the napkin. As soon as the pressure from the cloth was released, the cut across the knuckles began to bleed freely.

'That's one heck of a sharp door,' I said. The cut was paper thin, not bruised at all. 'Yup, you could guillotine cardboard with a door like that.'

'Just caught it wrong, I guess,' Boon laughed again.

'You need something on it – some dressing,' I said. 'Mind if I call a doctor?'

'Ah, no need to bother a doctor for a scratch,' he said. 'Can't we just ask reception for a first aid box? They'd probably have one here.'

'Place like this'd have its own ambulance,' Sissy suggested and headed for the phone.

'I say, would anybody mind telling me what's going on?' Khin asked.

Twenty minutes later the fingers were dressed and Khin was up to speed. Arny took a Coke from the mini-bar but we oldies sat around a bottle of Glenlivet. We'd already come to some agreement on Khin's value as an advisor on regional history but, in return, the director insisted on hearing the treasure hunt story. That one glass of whisky had loosened Khin's tongue. She happily blurted out her top-secret treasure tale and I began a not particularly simultaneous translation. Sissy filled the gaps on idioms and Khinisms I didn't get.

'Right off the bat,' Khin began, 'I am obliged to say that I shall not be sharing any of my wealth with you all.'

The listeners considered that fair.

'Very well, then,' she said. 'I shall begin with my sources; a prologue as it were. Most of the early history of the region was written on palm leaf by monks. In this climate, a good palm leaf manuscript could survive for around two hundred years. In that respect it is more reliable than paper. When the palm leaf begins to fade, the temple would take it upon itself to transcribe the history onto new palm leaf. Thus we have records that date back to the eleventh century.

'As there were many ethnic groups in the region, a number of languages were used – Mon, Shan and Burmese, to name but a few – and sometimes it was necessary for them to be translated from archaic scripts. Early scholars attempted to collect these records and collate them into what we refer to as chronicles. There were a number of notable chronicles in my country as well as your own. But there are thousands of palm leaf records scattered about willy-nilly in temples and only a fraction of them have been translated. Some of these are written in such obsolete scripts they might very well keep one scholar occupied for a lifetime.'

Khin gestured for us to refill her glass but Sissy held onto the bottle.

'Don't want you dropping off before the exciting part, old girl,' he said.

'Assuming there is an exciting part,' I added.

'Then I shall cut to the chase,' Khin continued. 'Where was I?'

'Translations,' said Arny who'd always been sucked in by Khin's stories.

'Quite so. One problem international scholars have is that my woebegone country has a … a little problem, politically.'

'Yeah, and World War Two was a scuffle,' Sissy laughed.

'To be more accurate, Burma is run by corrupt bastards,' said Khin. 'They don't facilitate access to historical data, not even to we researchers within the country. But since the student massacre of 88 and the subsequent closing of schools, I have been able, thanks to a small university discretionary fund, to sneak off into the Burmese countryside and conduct research of my own. It was as a result of these studies and my unbridled enthusiasm that I was finally given the go ahead to temporarily leave my country and coordinate matters in Thailand.'

'Khin!' I interrupted.

'I don' …Yes, Jimm?'

'Where's the chase?'

'I assure you it is just beyond the next hillock,' she said. 'Enter here, King Mangrai.'

'Come in grandpa,' Sissy pumped his fist in the air.

'King Mangrai was an exceedingly wealthy monarch,' said Khin. 'Apart from the natural gems and ores mined in his kingdom of Lanna, he received tribute from all those lesser kings around him. For his second, this time 'Sovereign' coronation perhaps at the turn of the thirteenth century, he received one hundred and eight priceless artifacts from the Vietnamese descendents of his own lineage to add to his official regalia. Mangrai was the last king of the Lao Chong succession and the first of the line naturally named after himself; the Mangrai dynasty. In curtailing their lineage he needed to pay tribute to the twenty four kings of the Ngoen Yang, or Tree of Silver, period of history that had preceded him. He needed to make an enormous sacrifice to their spirits.

'According to one of the Pagan chronicles he decided to bury the royal paraphernalia which included the ceremonial Sikanchai dagger - the Sword of Victory - and the royal spear, not to mention the one hundred and eight priceless artifacts, and dedicate it all to his father's ancestors. Thus the memory of the dynasty would remain intact. So it was that none of the crown jewels were mentioned again at subsequent Mangrai dynasty coronations despite the fact that a number of chronicles go into great detail of all the pomp and circumstance surrounding them.'

'And you think you know where they are?' Boon asked through me.

'I know where they should be,' said Khin. 'You see? They resurfaced at the end of the eighteenth century, sometime around 1790. By then my beloved Burma had seized Lanna and held it for over two hundred years.'

'Bastards,' Sissy mumbled.

'My humble apologies,' said Khin. 'But fear not. King Taksin of Bangkok decided to reclaim Lanna for Siam. His general for this task was called Kawila. To cut a very long story short, as the Burmese resources were rather thin on the ground due a slight altercation with invading British forces, Kawila was able to send our occupying troops back across the Salaween river with relative ease. He began to restore the deserted and almost ruined city of Chiang Mai to its former splendor. Taksin was so pleased with Kawila's efforts that he appointed him first ruler, then king of Lanna. At Kawila's coronation, what do you suppose made a return visit from the grave?'

Arny and I put up our hands but Khin continued unaided.

'The Sikanchai dagger and various other items of Mangrai's regalia, no less,' she said. 'It is mentioned in two chronicles that Kawila wished to recreate the glorious days of Lanna and allow the populace to see the paraphernalia of the great Lao Chong dynasty. I have no idea how they found the stuff but by all accounts it was an impressive collection. One of my main objectives in Thailand has been to track down the manuscript describing King Kawila's coronation day.'

Just like me and Arny the very first time we heard Khin's story, Boon was sucked in hook, line and sinker.

'So, Kawila used Mangrai's regalia but it didn't pass down through the rest of the dynasty,' he said, urging the story forward.

'No, that's just it,' said Khin. 'For several months after the coronation, there were accounts of widespread flooding around the soon-to-be-refurbished city of

Chiang Mai. There was unrest amongst a populace forcibly relocated to repopulate her. The flooding brought disease. Disaster fell upon disaster. Kawila's advisors reminded him of King Mangrai's intention to honour his ancestors by burying the treasure. They convinced him that by disinterring it they had riled the souls of the Lao Chong kings. There was only one way to placate the spirits.'

'Put it back in the ground,' said Arny.

'Exactly. There is no mention of the Sikanchai dagger being utilized in any of the subsequent coronations.'

'So, where is it?' asked Boon.

'Buried somewhere deep in his imagination,' I mumbled in Thai. Khin had reached her manic stage. There was no stopping her.

'Ah, and here we encounter difficulties,' she said. 'I'll make no bones about it. You see, Kawila didn't exactly leave a map with a cross on it.'

'Khin's heading out into the countryside with a metal detector after the movie,' said Sissy. I translated.

'That would be the equivalent of finding a needle in a haystack,' Khin confessed. 'In fact I should be able to narrow matters down considerably before push comes to shove. It was traditional to bury valuables in the base structure of temple stupas. There was an odd belief that we Burmese barbarians wouldn't think of looking there. In actual fact we had the same tradition ourselves. Given the importance of the swag, Kawila would have built a rather significant stupa to house it.'

'Then you think it's under one of the great temples here in Chiang Mai?' Boon asked.

'I doubt it,' said Khin, 'although it isn't totally out of the question. There was a good deal of building and renovating going on here at that time, but also a lot of eyes. A lot of spies. While they were waiting to move into the refurbished city, Kawila built a fortified encampment at Wieng Pa Sang, now known merely as Pa Sang. It's about twenty kilometers south. It grew into quite a bustling center. The area we are in was a leading world enclave of Buddhism for many centuries and religious edifices attached themselves to new settlements like leaches to a ripe buttock. It would not have been at all uncommon for such a place to be surrounded with temples. I'm betting my best skirt on one of those stupas being the final resting place of King Mangrai's treasure.'

'And a very pretty pink skirt it would be to lose,' said Sissy.

'It's Salmon,' said Khin. 'May I have a drink, now?'

'Certainly, Khin,' I smiled.

Arny poured her a generous glass of scotch and watched her squint as she took a sip.

'Okay, I'm sold,' Boon said.

'You are?' I said, amazed how easily even knowledgeable people were taken in by treasure stories. I could see the passion in Boon's eyes.

'Oh, I don't buy the reality,' he said, 'but it's a cracking story. I'll buy the rights off her.'

'I'm not sure a Burmese citizen can hold the rights to Thai history,' I said.

'Well, my guess is this has equal helpings of fiction and fact,' said Boon, 'so I'm just buying the tale. And tell her I'll fund her research for six more months. Let's see what other juice we can squeeze out of this mango.'

When the news reached Khin we detected a flicker of a smile on her lips.

'How much is he paying?' she asked.

We groaned but Boon thought it was a fair question. He took the notepad from the bedside table and wrote a figure.

'It won't be a Hollywood advance,' he said. 'I don't normally get to stay in places like this. But it should be enough to keep her in noodles.'

He passed the paper to Khin who managed an authentic Rangoon smile – the type that once lit up the streets of the Burmese capital before the gloom of oppression descended. She flashed the figure in our direction and we yelped with delight and wrestled the big embarrassed sack of bones down onto the bed and ruffled her well-combed hair.

It was 1AM by the time the amok runners left Boon's room. We'd woken Khin, still ruffled, five minutes earlier. We had the Thursday morning off because the next shoot would be at night. As we neared the lobby, I remembered my cloth shoulder bag and told the others I'd see them in the car park. Boon answered the door without his shirt.

'Sorry, forgot my bag,' I said. I walked past the director and into the room. 'How's your hand doing?'

'Good, I think. I'll let you know for certain when the whisky wears off.'

I hooked the bag strap over my shoulder and stood in the middle of the room.

'It wasn't the door,' I said.

'What?'

'Your hand. It wasn't the door. The bathroom door slides shut. It was a knife, and a pretty sharp one. Maybe even a razor.'

Boon let out a smile that had nothing to do with happiness. 'I don't ...'

'I'd bet one of them held you and the other one cut, one finger at a time,' I said. 'Backs of the knuckles, not much meat. Most people would be surprised how much it hurts when you run a blade over the bone. Aches like buggery.'

Boon and I locked gazes, neither speaking for a good twenty seconds. I broke the deadlock.

'If you need a friend,' I said.

'Yeah.'

'Or want to talk.'

'I appreciate it – really.'

'I'm not kidding.'

'I know.'

We walked to the door and Boon held it open for me.

'Thank you,' he said.

'See ya.'

'Jimm? How do you know so much about pain?'

'I work on the crime desk. People love to tell us how much things hurt.'

Chapter 4

**"Rough business, this movie business. I'm gonna
have to go back to loan-sharking just to take a
rest."**
Get Shorty. (1995)

A *kom fy* is a poor man's hot air balloon. It's about the
size of a fat lady's muumuu. It comprises a white tissue
paper cylinder with a closed top. At the bottom on a
cross-hatch of sticks or a wire frame, burns a small
wick. The flame warms the air inside until the creature
slowly ghosts into the night and floats like a
shimmering jellyfish on obliging currents of air. In
November, during the *Loi Gratong* festival, they turn the
sky over Chiang Mai into a mystical planetarium of
gently floating stars. Of course they also endanger
flights into Chiang Mai airport and burn down people's
houses but everyone agrees it's worth it for that inner-
warmth, that meditative calm that comes from lying on
your back and allowing your soul to swim amongst
them.

It would have taken a most perverse screenwriter on
holiday to envisage the lovely *kom fy* as a weapon of
mass destruction. But that's exactly what happened.
'What if?' someone had asked, 'What if you attach small
bags – pig's bladders, perhaps, filled with the sixteenth
century equivalent of Agent Orange? The flame burns
down to the string that harnesses the bag to the *kom fy*
and releases a deadly rain of toxic panic. The Burmese
below, intoxicated by the magic lanterns flying above
their heads, feel the light patter of rain. In seconds it

burns through their faces into their brains and leaves them running amok. There we have it.

They could add the lethal water bombs digitally but a computer could never emulate the majestic rise of a flock of *kom fy* at night. The filming location was a hillside behind the new Night Safari – one more peccadillo of the recently ousted prime-minister. The land had been slated for an elephant park and other sideshows in the premier's mega-plan to turn the quaint city into a Disneyland for the world's tourists. The vacuum of power following his ouster was a small blessing for the film makers. They were able to make small corrupt deals locally rather than enormously corrupt deals institutionally. The elephant parkland was ideal for this scene and the district headman even offered to remove the unsightly trees for a modest fee. Boon decided to keep the greenery.

Thousands of *kom fy* had been assembled and lit. It was a splendid sight and great cinema. When they launched the huge flotilla it was as if the luminous shell of the mountain had broken loose and set off in search of heaven. It was a moment that not one person present would be likely to forget. The Thai crew and extras secretly attached their blessings and dreams to a balloon. On film it would look spectacular but only those who felt their hearts rise with the *kom fy* could appreciate its all-powerful karma. Boon had visualized it – documented it. All agreed it would be his crowning achievement. If only the *kom fy* had not been on a mission of destruction. If only the launching had been a symbol of hope, it could have been one of cinema's most poignant moments.

Sissy and I cried as we watched the mountain rise into the sky.

But Friday was the day the spirit of the desecrated *kom fy* ceremony began to wreak its revenge. Everything had gone so well that week. Khin left for Pa Sang that morning. She planned to visit the temples around the area but wasn't about to destroy the stupas brick by ancient brick. Her intention was to recover her treasure academically. She would tick off the clues one by one and arrive there logically – not with a pick or a shovel but with a key – a cognitive key crafted of her own brilliance.

She still carried a letter from Chiang Mai University: *'The bearer of this document is Ms. Khin Thein Aye. She is conducting important historical research in collaboration with this university and the dean of the faculty of humanities requests your cooperation in allowing her access to historical manuscripts and artifacts in your possession.'* It was signed and stamped and carried all the stuffy authority of a Thai University letter.

Khin could have said all this herself; one word at a time over a period of a day. She spoke, last count, six regional dialects and read another six languages. But there was something about her aversion to Thai tones and the frustration she'd encountered trying to get people to understand her in Thailand that suggested she'd reached 'full' on the language tank gauge.

The American armada was due to land the following day. Perhaps that was why an even gloomier smog than usual descended upon the north of Thailand. It clouded moods and eclipsed the last of the sunny dispositions.

There is a Thai word – *sanook*. It doesn't have an exact English counterpart. It encompasses a number of states; fun, relaxation of rules, enjoyment – but none of these terms really hit it. It's better described by its absences; of pressure, of control, of inhibition; and when the heavies arrived from Hollywood that weekend, all those negatives made landfall with them. Movie-making became work. The atmosphere became denser and harder to breathe in.

The big guns took over the Dhara Dhevi and booked it for ten days. OB, the director, had a suite. Oliver Benjamin was currently on a roll. Everything he touched turned to butts on seats. Four consecutive hits and no sign of letting up. He could choose his projects and ask however the hell much he wanted – and get it. The producers knew they'd recoup it. The roses hadn't always smelled so sweet in OB's forty-year career so he was strolling and taking the moments to savor the bouquet.

Dan "the teeth" Jensen had a suite. He arrived with his crew, manager, makeup, personal trainer, voice coach, publicist, sexily slutty female 'friend', and someone to carry the shih tzu. There might have been a gofer too and a couple of hangers-on but the awe-struck receptionist lost count. If a studio took on Dan Jensen they took on his baggage. It was in the contract. He was worth it. Just by taking off his shirt in a movie he could add fourteen million to the take. There were those who believed he could act but it was his unruly ash blond hair and perfect dentures that got him through most scenes.

Bunny Savage had a suite. The entourage that rode her particular fame was smaller; manager, publicist, makeup, and a Jewish bodyguard, Gus, built like the Wailing Wall. Savage was newly hot. She'd rocketed to stardom on the back of a TV sitcom and the fact she had a figure to melt granite. She'd probably learn to ride the studios some day but right now she was a steal at fifteen million for ten days location and another month of studio work back in California. The bellboy tripped over his tongue showing her to the room.

There were other actors, producers, the assistant director, the line director, the head cinematographer and so, ad infinitum. Well-heeled Thais and mere millionaires had no chance of fighting their way into the Dhara Dhevi for the next ten days. Hollywood set up its beach head during the day while Sissy, our team and I used up the last of our *sanook*. Boon had been with us in the morning for a few mop-up sitting-around-doing-culturally-appropriate-things shots. The afternoon was close-ups of glaring eyes, hands on swords, sandaled feet trudging through rice fields, muscles glistening with sweat – a whole picture board of just-in-case inserts for OB to choose from. Boon had left his head cameraman to take care of these and driven off into the city for some important appointment – we assumed with OB. Before he left he'd asked us about Khin's progress and wished us all well.

The first week unit sat around looking at the digital version of the day's shoots, applauding themselves and Boon's vision. During the day, more and more intruders had trampled over our *sanook*. Stateside experts had strolled onto the set and made unwanted suggestions to the Thai film team. Observers had begun to gather like the ominous birds in the Hitchcock thriller. It was the end of the party. From now on the amok runners would blend in, be heads in crowds, drilled battlefield troops, or bodies. If we hadn't been identifiable in a close up by now we knew we never would be. Two thousand new extras were being recruited over the weekend by a different agency. The machine had arrived and we weren't even cogs any more.

As we were walking away from the final showing, a large man in a sweat-stained brown shirt and a Greg Norman monogrammed straw hat approached us. He ignored me and Sissy and put his hand on Arny's shoulder. The man didn't introduce himself.

'How'd you like to make yourself another five hundred *baht* a day, boy?' he asked.

'Does it involve him touching you in intimate places?' I asked, knowing Arny was too soft and sweet to make such a crack.

The man thought for a second then a stunned expression fell across his face.

'Hell, no! What'd you think I am? Hell, no. I'm a Christian. I have a wife and three beautiful children. Shit.'

He spoke with such alarm in his voice that I knew for sure the guy had a desire, innate or otherwise, to be touched in intimate places by another man. I let it ride.

'Then what are you offering?' I asked.

'What are you, his agent?' he asked.

'I'm his sister,' I said. 'What do you want him for?'

'Stand in. Know what that is?'

'Yup,' said Sissy.

'What's a stand in?' Arny asked.

The sweaty man's eyebrows sprang toward his hairline. I guessed he hadn't expected the locals to have minds.

'You find a guy the same size as one of the actors,' Sissy explained in English, 'and have him stand around so the cameras can set up. Sometimes they shoot your back or film you from a distance so the star can have more time back in his trailer snorting coke.'

'Hey. We don't have any of that on our movies,' said the sweaty guy.

'Yeah, right,' I said.

'I don't know,' said Arny.

'It sure beats third row from the back,' I told him.

'Not really,' said Sissy. 'I did it for Tom Berenger in the Sniper movie. It wasn't a lot of fun. You're on your own.'

'I'd sooner be back there with you guys,' said Arny.

'There aren't any 'you guys' after this weekend,' I reminded him. 'Khin's off chasing her crackpot treasure and me and Sissy will be drowned in a sea of black hair. You'd be somebody up here. Do it.'

'Yeah,' said Arny. 'I don't know.' He turned to the sweaty guy. 'Who'd I be standing in for?'

'Dan Jensen,' said the guy.

'He'll do it,' Sissy told him. 'And, yes, I'm his agent.'

Chapter 5

**"It happens to everybody, horses, dogs, men.
Nobody gets out of life alive."**
Hud (1965)

I arrived at Khin's house just as the sun began to roll over the back of the mountain and the dog chorus howled the end of another day. The trees all around held off most of the sun but it was still hot as Hades inside that big glass-doored people aquarium. I'd been staying with Khin for a week just to get away from the shop and Mair's nuttiness and granddad Ja's bad moods. At thirty-three I was too old to still be living at home but I couldn't afford to live by myself. I'd tried marriage and that didn't work, probably because I'd gone at it as a form of escape. Sissy had her own place and I'd stay with him when the family got to me. Even with its lack of privacy, Khin's house provided me with a retreat. Families are awful things.

I rolled three inappropriately small T-shirts and a spare pair of jeans and put them in my pack. Two pairs of panties, shorts, bras, socks and running shoes and I was all set. The next day we'd be off 'on location'. Left to my own devices I probably wouldn't have chosen Fang to get away to, but for reasons none of the amok runners could fathom that's where the bulk of the movie was to be shot. It was the wild north – some pretty scenery but politically and socially out of control.

I was changing into something more conducive to lounging when I found the fliers the LA people had handed out that afternoon. I lit a mosquito coil, placed it under the beach recliner and turned on the outside light. The first sheet was a press handout with a synopsis of the movie. Everyone knew it was a rip off of 'The Last Samurai'. Americans loved the idea of sending their boys off to mend broken countries in the developing world. I read it aloud in my James Earl Jones voice.

'SIAM. It is the year 1560 and the sovereign of the Siamese kingdom of Lanna faces a lamentable end for his people at the hands of the cruel and vengeful Burmese hordes.'

I smiled and sipped a tonic water, imagining Khin's reaction.

'A prolonged fifty-year war against the invaders has left the Thai monarch low on resources and hope. In desperation he writes to his old friend, Lee, in the free world and explains his plight. (Lee?) Lee has fought beside the brave frontiersmen taming the savage continent of America. He has earned the trust and friendship of their leader, Andrew Axeman, the son of an English Lord unjustly banished to the Americas. Upon hearing Lee's story, and valuing brotherhood above all, Axeman sets off with his band of fearless fusiliers to rescue Siam from tyranny.

Although Axeman earns the respect of the Lanna monarch and wins the love of a beautiful Shan princess, will his brand of forest warfare, taught to him by his father on their family estate in Suffolk, be enough to outsmart the powerful Burmese army?

This true story plucked from the cobwebs of time tells of a man who traveled to the far corners of the earth to ensure the triumph of good over evil; an unsung hero of America's distant past. This is a story of everything that makes our nation great, of wisdom, of determination, of ...'

I was feeling too nauseous to read on. I let out a helpless simian screech. A gibbon up on the slopes replied. There was so much wrong with the hand-out I couldn't even begin to lambast it. Expecting worse, I scanned the second sheet. It was a cast list with colour photos – the type you might find in a theatre programme. The pictures deliberately homed in on the parts of the celebrity you were supposed to admire. OB, the director, shot from above so you saw mostly cranium. Seventy something and good-looking. A big, grey skull. The brain of the operation.

Then there was Jensen, Andrew Axeman himself. A third of the picture was smile. The hint of a bare shoulder intimating that the rest of him might be naked. Heaven help us. But I had to admit to a little shudder of lust. Then there was the director's muse, the Savage rabbit, the babe. Bunny wore a low-cut V-neck cashmere sweater. Her focal points nestled in there nicely. Nice face, misleadingly pensive. I doubted much thought went through that pretty head.

Next face down was King Maeku, the Thai monarch-under-siege, played, of course, by Yasue Kuro, a samurai movie star gone inter. Thai, Japanese – same difference to Edna in South Chicago. His exotic mail-slot eyes glared handsomely from the photo. Thai King Mongkut had been played with varying degrees of incredulity by a Russian, Yul Brynner, and a Chinese, Yun-Fat Chow, so why not a Japanese? Heaven forbid Hollywood might cast a Thai in the role. Given the lust for celebrity they'd probably ask Tiger Woods. Casting was all about popularity and little to do with acting ability. There had been talk of Paris Hilton playing the Shan princess but Bunny Savage's dark Italian features made her a more credible Asian.

Of the other eight or so main stars there was one Thai. Just one. He was Chucheep Ongsagul, recognized by the royal household as a National Artist in the field of the performing arts. He had a fifty-year career on stage and in films. At the bottom of the cast list was his name, misspelled, and his role: a villager.

More distant dogs barked long before I heard the engine of the Caribbean throb up to the house. A few minutes later, Sissy was standing beside the recliner.

'Hello bro,' I said. 'You seen these yet?'

I held up the fliers but Sissy ignored them and loomed over me like an undertaker.

'Jimm,' he said. 'You've really gotta turn your phone on sometime.'

'What's up?

'Director Boon. He's dead.'

The tonic water had necessarily given way to Saeng Thip rum. It was nasty but it was the only booze Khin had in the house. We sat facing each other while Sissy detailed everything he knew about the killing. When Boon left the set earlier that day he'd driven into town. He'd parked his rental car in the lot at the back of Doi Chang coffee shop on Nimanhemin. It wasn't clear whether he'd planned to meet someone at the coffee shop or walk on somewhere else because he was shot four meters from his car. Two bullets, both to the head. No witnesses.

'Say something,'

'I'm thinking,' I said.

'The cops said it sounded like a typical hit. They found motorcycle tracks in the dirt by the body. They said it was probably …'

'… a business-related conflict,' I said.

'Yeah.'

That's what they always say.'

'Yup.'

'It makes it neater. Nobody feels sorry for you if you screw up in business.'

'I know.'

'Remember the safari shirts in the lobby at the Dhara Dhevi?'

'I've been thinking about them.'

'Think they were police?'

'It's possible.'

'If they were police ...'

'Don't do this again, Jimm.'

'All I'm saying is if the guys that threatened Boon on Wednesday were police I can't really see the cops being too transparent in investigating his death. Can you?'

'Jimm? You're a reporter.'

'A crime reporter.'

'As opposed to a private detective. Don't get us involved in another one of your cases.'

'We are involved. We're witnesses to intimidation.'

'It might not be connected,' said Sissy.

'You know it is.'

'And who do you suppose we tell? Unless you've got friends at Interpol there's not a thing you can do about it.'

'We'll just keep our eyes open is all I'm saying.'

'I heard that before.'

'Serious. Just observe.'

'Right.'

Chapter 6

"We had two bags of grass, seventy-five pellets of mescaline, five sheets of high-powered blotter acid, a saltshaker half-full of cocaine and a whole galaxy of multi-colored uppers, downers, screamers, laughers ... Also, a quart of tequila, a quart of rum, a case of beer, a pint of raw ether and two dozen amyls. Not that we needed all that for the trip, but once you get locked into a serious drug collection, the tendency is to push it as far as you can."

Fear and Loathing in Las Vegas (1998)

The city of Fang was established as a formal trading settlement by prodigious old King Mangrai during his heyday. He'd probably be sorry at the way it turned out. It loomed like a disappointing oasis at the end of a long flat drive from the foot of the Chiang Dao mountains. Not even the optimists of Lonely Planet could find a kind word for it. A stubborn hairpin bend after the river was the only reason passing traffic slowed down long enough to take it in at all. There were three hotels that seemed to say, 'Why the hell would you want to stay in Fang?' one or two roadside restaurants where the food benefited from the carbon monoxide, and a Seven-Eleven. Even dumps had a Seven-Eleven in twenty-first century Thailand.

But Fang was the administrative centre for the region and it didn't pretend to be anything it wasn't. Most of the traffic just kept on going along route 107 in the direction of Chiang Rai. Sissy and I had stayed the night at Khin's and swung by the shop to pick up Arny. Mair was still sulking about her debacle. We'd driven

49

the two hours north in the jeep marvelling how the old jalopy was still able to climb hills. The film unit had invaded an area north of the city called Tha Ton. It was a fairly picturesque part of the country with calendar mountains and a slow moving river called the Kok. The town itself comprised a bridge, a police kiosk and several spidery lanes running parallel to the river. The pier was the launch point for long-tail boat or raft trips to Chiang Rai up near the Burmese border.

Looming over this tiny hub was the Tha Ton temple mountain topped with a glittery stupa with its very own Hollywood sign. The words WAT THA TON CRYSTAL CHEDI stood in large plasterboard Thai characters legible from the surrounding hills. An albino Buddha sat in meditation below it. Rather than share their wealth with the poor or rescue crippled animals, Thai Buddhists preferred to donate their money to stuff. Many spent their income on bizarrely opulent whims: a mirrored archway, a whole team of gold-plated Buddhas and celebrity monks, bells and dragons, concrete boats, and ten-foot captions.

Gangs of Akha hill-tribe women in clinking headdresses roamed the streets of Tha Ton and lighted upon hapless foreigners, bullying them into buying embroidery. There were garlic drying sheds and small bamboo treatment foundries all around and the ongoing sound of machetes. There was no shortage of noises and sights but nothing recommended the town more than the fact that it could, at a squeeze, accommodate three-hundred actors and crew. There was one hotel called the Chalet, two sets of bungalows which had the nerve to call themselves resorts, and half a dozen guest houses. Despite Arny's new standing as a stand-in and the offer of high-end accommodation, he'd opted to stay with me and Sissy at the Garden Home. We'd stayed there before. It was a collection of wooden huts neatly spaced amid a sort of botanical experiment. It was as if the owners were more interested in the garden than in the guests. The rooms were barely larger than tool sheds and only three had views of the river. We'd phoned ahead to reserve one of these for our ten days in Tha Ton.

The Chalet was certainly the top end in town but it was a distant dark star from the brilliance of the Dhara Dhevi. OB and the stars were billeted at the former but it was unlikely they'd use the little rooms for much more than changing and naps. There were no suites, spas or pools but each room had four thousand BTU of air, free stationery, and all four local TV stations. For people like Dan Jensen it was a hardship posting in the third world. He'd walked into the room, laughed, and walked out. A police helicopter had been negotiated to shuttle the upper echelons of stardom back to their ivory tower in Chiang Mai after the day's shoots. We felt Jensen would spend more time on that chopper than most.

Just out of Tha Ton was the project site. The set designers had recreated a corner of olde Chiang Mai out of plaster and foam. Its ramparts and the city moat looked just like the artist's impression at the museum. Within the walls were temples and markets and an arena for cockfights. At the other end of the valley were the royal palace and a number of picturesque gardens where characters would meet and conspire and frolic. It was all as historically accurate as the researchers could make it but it looked so marvellous nobody really cared. On the far side of the mountain was the gently sloping plain chosen for the final confrontation; the almighty battle between the Burmese and the besieged Siamese. It gave me a full-on buzz just walking around the set.

'It's a kick, though, man,' said Sissy in New Yorkian.

With a little dark blush to his chin and his breast binding, my brother looked more like a man than I'd ever seen him.

'It gets into your blood, doesn't it?' I agreed.

Arny had been smiling all day. We sat on our ramshackle balcony with our feet on the rail. The Kok river, pigeon grey and lethargic, flowed by just a few meters from the cabin.

'I can see why you do it,' Arny told Sissy.

'There's a lot of sitting around,' he replied, 'but … I don't know. There's something about being involved in it. We grew up going to the movies and watching Mair's old Beta cassettes. It's always been my fall-back fantasy world. You don't have to be a big part of it. Just hold onto its skirt and follow it around. At the time you don't feel the real magic but you sense it. Then you go and see the movie and all the pieces are fitted together and you're up there on the screen. You probably won't even get close enough to nod hello to the stars but when that movie's out it's … "So, me and Dan Jensen just made this movie in Fang …"'

'Hello?' came a voice.

'We're out back,' I yelled.

Our's wasn't the most sprawling of residences. Visitors had little trouble circumnavigating it. The sweaty man, still wearing his Greg Norman hat and still damp at eight-thirty at night, arrived first.

'Ah, there you are,' he said. 'Can't think why you're staying out here in the middle of nowhere.'

A few paces back was a figure I recognized. The grey hair had turned tropical and sprung off at all angles. It made that big skull look like a photo of a kapok mattress exploding. The guy from the flier – the cranium – was a pace behind his gofer.

'OB wants to get a look at your boy,' sweaty said.

We raised our hands in a most respectful *wai*. I discretely stood in front of the joint that puffed guiltily on the wooden deck. It was like being busted by the school principal.

'Hi, guys,' said OB. 'I'm Oliver Benjamin.'

'How you doing?' I said

'Hi, OB,' said Sissy. Arny just stood there with his mouth open.

'This one's Arny,' Sweaty said without any real need. Our brother was the only one vaguely resembling the muscle-bound Jensen. In fact, Arny was more everything than Jensen himself.

'I just wanted to check you out, see how you look from the rear,' OB said, stepping up onto the deck.

'He gets a lot of old guys checking out his rear end,' I said before giving myself a few seconds to think about it. 'I'm not saying you're old or anything. It was just …'

'Well done, Jimm.' Sissy clapped. 'Not yet on the job and you get us fired.'

But OB seemed to enjoy the comment. He had a gravelly laugh that spoke of cigarettes of yore. He was tanned more from working outdoors than George Hamilton vanity and he had a good set of teeth, too comfortable in his mouth to be fake. He was a good looking guy in his seventies; at ease and worldly. We had Arny stand and turn a slow pirouette making sure to wiggle his butt on the way round.

'Hope I'm not a disappointment,' said Arny.

'For fear of further ridicule,' OB smiled, 'now I'm reluctant to ask you to take off your shirt.'

Sissy snorted a laugh. 'And maybe a quick peak at your pecker?' he said.

Arny blushed.

Sweaty stepped in. 'No call for that kind of talk.'

OB laughed again. 'That's okay. We aren't doing the porn version till this one goes to video. Just a look at your back'll be good.'

Arny stripped off his shirt and did his musical muscle man routine. He really was an impressive looking man.

'Wanna see mine?' Sissy asked.

'No, I think that'll do just fine, son,' said OB. He turned to the sweaty man, 'Thanks, Larry. I need to ask a few questions here. I'll find my own way back.'

'You sure, OB?'

'Sure. Night, Larry.'

Larry loped off to build up his sweat reserves and left the second biggest grossing movie director in Hollywood swaying from foot to foot on our deck.

'You want to sit down?' I asked.

OB nodded and the rattan seat creaked beneath him.

'We don't have a mini-fridge so the best we can offer's lukewarm water,' Sissy told him.

OB smiled. 'So, how long do you think you can keep that joint alight? At best you'll burn down the cabin.'

Sissy dived to his knees to rescue the weed. He blew at the fat end and brought it back to life.

'Sissy's got this fear of authority figures,' I told him and he laughed.

'It's a habit I picked up from our grandfather,' said Sissy. 'He's always sneaking around trying to catch us doing something sinful.'

I offered the joint to OB.

'Hmm. Don't mind if I do. I love that smell,' said the director, taking it respectfully between his thumb and index finger. He puffed and an expression crossed his face that suggested not a few of those seventy years had seen happy dope moments.

'You suppose Damp Larry got a whiff?' Sissy asked.

'Who cares?' said OB. 'You could be sitting here toasting weapons' grade plutonium on a spit and he'd keep his mouth shut. He gets paid too much to care about stuff he shouldn't.'

Half an hour later we were on the third of what OB called, doobees. Most of the lights of the town were out and the river slicked past black and oily. The natural sounds of the riverbank; frogs and cicadas and the like, reminded me how noisy nature could be. The conversation was loud but easy.

'So, did you miss the chopper?' I asked OB.

'Not exactly,' he said. 'The studio booked us into that museum playground in Chiang Mai but I can't say it's very convenient. This way I get an earlier start and I don't have to listen to The Teeth giving me advice on how to make a movie.'

'I take it you aren't so fond of our Dan,' said Sissy.

'There's always one on a set who believes everything their publicist puts out about them,' said OB. 'But this one, I tell you, he's weird. I get the feeling he was taking prima donna classes long before he hit the big time. You know what I'm saying? Got the spoiled-brat image down long before his first movie. If he listened to direction he could be an okay actor but he sulks and has his tantrums and walks out. You've just got to let him do his thing and hope he stumbles onto something worth filming. It's like being an animal trainer for a fish.'

'What are we doing here, OB?' Sissy asked.

'You mean philosophically?' he asked.

'No, physically. What are we doing in Fang?'

'It's pretty.'

'Thailand's got more pretty than you've got movie stories. Why are you filming here and not some easier place?'

'You don't think it's easy here?'

'OB,' I said, 'we're ten miles from the Burmese border in a place that was the drug running depot for the Golden triangle for fifty-odd years. All the wealth and power up here is a result of being a better hoodlum than the next guy. You could have set up almost anywhere else and made life less stressful on yourself.'

'Jimm, I don't have to think of any of that stuff,' he said. 'I make movies. The studio hires people to make decisions on location. I just nod agreement when they show me the video.'

'So, who recommended Fang?' Sissy asked.

'We have a Hong Kong office that hired a local company in Bangkok. They came out scouting locations together.'

'Do you know the name of the Bangkok company?'
I asked.

Sissy looked at me, 'Do we really need to know
that?' he said still hoping I wouldn't be investigating
any more than I was getting paid for.

'Sure we do,' I said. 'What kind of cool job would
that be? Getting paid to drive around and take videos
of mountains.'

'Star something,' OB said. 'Star Casting and …
Location? That kind of thing. I can ask my gofer
tomorrow.'

'Thanks.'

It hadn't taken OB long to dissolve into a mellow
state, dropping names and telling secrets. We'd hung
out with two big directors in the space of four days and
both of them had been 'real'. Except one of them was
now real and dead, and none of us could get that fact
out of our minds. When the roach pin was back in
Sissy's pocket we walked OB along the coal black lane
to his hotel. We felt responsible for him. We had to do
whatever we could to keep the curse in its box.

Chapter 7

"Yes, you have a great body. May I use it?"
Saturn 3 (1980)

Dan Jensen was a high-flying star and that gave him the right to stand up three hundred extras and crew on a whim. The word had returned on the empty helicopter that the actor had been unhappy with the breakfast muesli and there'd been an altercation at the buffet. It was unclear as to whether the dispute had led to fisticuffs, but the fact remained that Jensen was too disturbed to begin shooting that morning. He'd retired to his room with his disciples and was meditating with a corporate guru. Whatever the actual story, the sun was fighting its way free of the morning mist and Siam had no Andrew Axeman. OB decided to shoot around his scenes and insert them later. This however meant more work for Arny.

When you have ten days to stay within a budget you don't waste good sunlight, and nobody could honestly claim to have seen much of the sun before today. Their advisors should have warned the studio about March in the north but nobody could have predicted just how bad the pollution would be that year. The Chiang Mai authorities had announced sweeping measures to rescue the tourist industry from the smog. One of these involved the firing of hoses into the air downtown. Another was a plan to bring forward the Songkran water throwing festival by two weeks. But, as much of the smog originated from the junta on the Burmese side burning down forests to plant cash crops there wasn't much hope.

As the Thai military government had adopted a policy of not making any decisions during their tenure, the state of emergency announcement didn't materialize. Farmers continued to burn off their crops and trucks continued to clog up the Chiang Mai basin with their illicit emissions. Everyone waited lump in throat for the monsoon winds to come early and blow it all away. It was a particularly Buddhist approach to handling an environmental disaster.

Rather than wait for a sunny day, OB decided to turn the whole movie into something bleak and mysterious. He spent several hours with Arny filming over-the-shoulder and long-distance shots of the stand-in's back. The stylist had taken an hour to make his hair look like he'd just woken up but when she was through the back of his head was remarkably similar to Dan Jensen's. After watching a few minutes of old footage Arny had even been able to master the Dan Jensen amble. OB joked that he was tempted to shoot the whole movie with Arny and leave Jensen to his muesli wars. The director was enjoying his day without the star.

The only downside was that Andrew Axeman insisted on wearing his lucky buffalo-hide top coat. For a military campaign in the tropics one would have to question the frontiersman's sanity.

'This here coat was made by my ma for my pa (The young Lord Axeman had evidently dumbed down substantially since leaving Suffolk) and it was passed on to me. This coat's killed a whole messa injuns.'

Although the wardrobe people had done a splendid job of making cotton look like hide, the jacket was long-sleeved and high-necked and stifling in the humidity of Fang. Arny spent most of his walkthroughs bare-chested.

He was a stand-in, and nobody bothers to tell the stand-in anything. That's why he was shocked to see Bunny Savage appear on the set that afternoon. Perhaps Shan princesses really did dress like go-go dancers in the sixteenth century. They had researchers to ascertain such things. Perhaps Siamese kings did allow their concubines to walk around the palace with their bosoms hanging out and their g-stringed backsides visible beneath a sheer mesh miniskirt.

It would probably help here to recap my brother Arny's attitude towards sex. He wasn't having any of it. He was such a dreamboat he could have had his choice. He was the strong silent type and women of all ages found that endearing about him. But he refused point blank to bed anyone until he was in love and engaged to be married. We had no idea where that attitude came from, especially not from our mother who produced us out of wedlock and was seen on the arm of a battalion of gentlemen friends. Arny was painfully shy and soft spoken and, I'm loath to say, a bit of a wimp. We doubted he'd ever be able to woo a girl without backup. So it was lucky the scene that afternoon involved a group of villagers which included Sissy as a rugged carpenter. When the actress walked down the palace steps several hundred hearts, including those of two transvestite makeup artistes, came to a standstill. She was a poacher of breath, a purloiner of rational thought. Even Sissy caught himself staring at her with his tongue unfurled. What a sight. Eyes like pools of chocolate inviting every man to take the plunge. The borderline Botox/mother-nature lips. The wind-tunnel tested bone structure. The legs, the chest, the shoulders; more desirous than any woman had the right to be. It was all Sissy could do not to say, 'Wow, if only I had all that.' The only disconcerting aspect about her physical appearance was the bloody shaft of an arrow protruding from her kidney. It didn't seem to slow her down at all. She waved at OB and went to Arny with her hand held in front of her.

'Hello,' she said. 'I'm Bunny Savage.'

Her smile seemed to dribble hot mercury down the inside of his stomach. He took hold of her fingertips and squeezed them – more of a nail inspection than a handshake. His mouth was still open but nothing came out. Arny was struck dumb.

'You do speak English?' she asked.

'Little bit,' he managed.

'Then you're supposed to say, 'Pleased to meet you. I'm Jim'.'

'No,' said Arny.

'No what?'

'Jimm's my sister.'

Her smile grew larger, more real somehow – more intimidating.

'Then how about you substitute it for some other name? Like yours for example.'

'Arny,' said Arny.

That actually made her laugh.

'No connection to Schwarzenegger?'

'He's my hero.'

'Don't.'

'Honestly.'

Sissy could see his brother was struggling so he went to help.

'His real name's Arnon,' said Sissy.

'And who are you?' she asked.

'Sissy. I'm his brother.'

'And your name's Sissy?'

'Yup.'

'You know that has another meaning in my country?'

'You don't say.'

Sissy was about to add the fact that he was generally a woman but time constraints were against him. Quirk, the assistant director jogged up to them. He had two speeds, scurry and freeze. He was an out-of-shape Australian plucked from the spare director pool at the last minute when the original choice found God and vanished onto a retreat. Quirk filled the on-set asshole role and left no doubt as to why he was available at such short notice. He stood in front of Arny and Bunny but spoke with OB over his headset.

'You both know what's expected of you,' Quirk said. 'So I want you ...'

'No,' Arny shook his head.

'No, what?' said Quirk.

'No, I don't know what I'm doing.'

Quirk glared, angrily. 'Then I suggest you read the day's shooting schedule, mate.'

'Nobody's given me a shooting schedule,' said Arny.

He was very calm and non-accusing but he obviously rubbed the assistant director up the wrong way.

'Well, Mr. would-be Dan Jensen, you aren't gonna be a big star if you don't learn to read a schedule.'

He noticed Sissy as if for the first time.

'What are you doing here?'

'Looking manly and rugged,' said Sissy.

'Well go and do it over there with the hired help,' said Quirk.

'I don't,' said Arny.

'Don't what?' said Quirk.

'I don't want to be Dan Jensen.'

Bunny laughed. 'Okay gentlemen, break it up. John, I think I can explain the scene to Mr. Arny here.'

Quirk squeezed his earlobe and got his fingers caught in his earphone.

'Ms. Savage,' he said, 'when you've been in the business as many years as me, you'll find there's just some people you can't teach.'

He ran off to organize the extras.

'He's a dick head,' said Bunny. She had a way of making it sound erotic.

'Can't blame him,' Sissy smiled. His smile was probably the only part of my brother that hadn't aged with time. He was a good looking man but too wrinkly and broad-jawed to be called glamorous as a woman any more.

'The production company's under a lot of pressure from the IDF to hire people like that,' he said.

'International …?'

'… Dickhead Federation.'

Her laugh was bubbly.

'I see you're doing everything you can to hang onto this job,' she said. 'Any more of you at home?'

'One sister,' said Sissy.

'And what's her name?'

'Jimm.'

'Of course. I should have known.'

Sissy smiled and imagined himself and this new girl friend smoking joints and exchanging make-up tips on the deck.

'So,' she said. 'We're all bonded now. Arny, here's the deal. I don't know if you've noticed but I've got a bloody arrow sticking out of my gut.'

'Yes,' said Arny.

'So, anyway. I'm dying. You get to carry me into the …'

'Carry you?'

'That's right.'

'How much do you weigh?'

'Not much. It's not important. Just bend your knees.'

It was important in a way. Arny had the scar of a herniated disc operation from two months earlier as testament to how relevant it might be. All those years of lifting metal bars had taken its toll on his back. But, hell. Bunny Savage in his arms? Wasn't that worth a lifetime in a wheelchair?

'You're right,' he said. 'I'll do it.'

'Nice of you.'

In fact it took eight takes; change of camera angle, the damn sun making an appearance and screwing up the lighting, and Arny staggering into an urn. It was almost as if …

'Hey, mate. Are you deliberately trying to fuck this up?' Quirk shouted. He was passing the question on from OB who sat atop a tower of scaffold. Arny was sweating like a land eel and it was just as well they were only filming him from the back because he couldn't get that pained smile off his lips. Here he was walking around the sixteenth century with a beautiful woman in his arms. His back ached like a curse from Hell but Sissy had to admire the fact our little brother was going to make this scene last as long as he damn-well could.

They talked a lot between takes. Sissy breaking protocol each time and deserting his fellow tradesmen to chat with the star. Bunny wanted to know about Thailand and the effects of the October coup. They were surprised in a pleasant kind of way, not only that she'd be interested but that she might even be aware there'd been one. Sissy wished there were standing-in-front-of-tank anecdotes to tell but it had been a calm overnight takeover. The Prime Minister had been in the States and the military strolled into parliament and announced they were in charge. There were no shots fired and the overall opinion in Chiang Mai seemed to be that the general couldn't do any worse than the previous guy. Bunny Savage took it all in but left Sissy with the impression she'd be asking others to get a balanced view.

My brothers were equally surprised when they tried to tell her about the Shan of whom she was a surrogate representative in the movie. She began a recitation she'd memorized.

'The Shan,' she said. 'Inhabitants of Shan State in northern Burma since before the thirteenth century, probably migrants from China. Often the historical whipping boys for the big bully kingdoms around them. At one time a part of the Chiang Mai Lanna realm. More recently, brutalized and displaced by the oppressive Burmese junta. Their culture presently in danger from a series of dams being built along the Salween River.'

My brothers stared into her chocolate eyes.

'Gee, you do your homework,' said Arny.

'I know a lot more,' she said. 'I've been passing it on in press interviews but I doubt they'll print it. Not sexy enough. I have a secretary who finds these things out for me.'

'Did she do the research on fifteenth century Shan costumes, too?' Sissy asked.

Bunny smiled.

'No. I'm guessing that was the decision of some dirty old man in marketing. I fought against it.'

'Can't say too many of the boys here are sorry you lost.'

Finally, feeling marginally bad about all the dollars he'd helped waste, Arny gritted his teeth and strode manfully to the deathbed with his Shan princess in his arms. He had one final squeeze, lay her on the Thai silk sheets and the ominous sound of 'cut, that's a wrap' broke the silence behind him. It was all over. Sissy came over to pat his brother on the back. He looked down at the unconscious princess, blood oozing erotically from a plastic pouch in her breastplate.

'Should I get you a doctor?' he asked.

'I pull through,' said Bunny. 'I've read the script.'

'That's a relief. We had a good time today.'

'Yes we did,' said Arny.

'There's obviously not much going on in your lives,' she smiled.

Despite all Sissy's instincts and proclivities to dislike 'a woman like her', she'd crawled in under his 'poser' radar. Yes, they could be girlfriends.

'We have a family cabin down at the Garden Home,' he told her. 'It's a bunch of bungalows covered in weeds. We sit on the balcony and talk shit most nights. If you miss the chopper and feel like a cup of tea …'

'Thanks.'

He got it in a fraction of a second before the sycophants came flooding over her. He and Arny were the losing boxer in the ring, nudged out and pushed onto the ropes. They caught a glimpse of her amid the scrum and then she was gone. They might spot her on a cliff overlooking the battle or get to cheer Axeman as he sweeps her into his arms, but their personal moment had passed.

Chapter 8

"No-one ever leaves a star. That's what makes one a star."
Sunset Boulevard (1950)

When I arrived back from the beheading at the central market I found Arny flat on his back on the cabin deck, still wearing his frontiersman jacket open to the navel. He was reading a romance novel held at arm's length in front of his face. There was a hot-water thermos and a teapot on the side table. I sat beside him on the ground.

'Rough day, dear?'

'I don't want to talk about it,' said Arny. 'How was yours?'

'I don't know how they ever get a movie made,' I said. 'I swear I don't. It took them six hours just to cut a guy's head off.'

'What did they use, nail clippers?'

That was a rare Arny joke that I chose to ignore so I could give full sail to my whinging.

'A sword,' I said. 'Big motherfriggin Sinbad the Sailor sword. You think it'd be easy. Woosh! Clunk! All over. But, oh no; they drag the guy in, set it all up, do the lines, we all freeze in position, they bring on the fake guy, put him in the right spot and cut his phony head off. How hard can it be? Then the sound guy tells us there was a frigging airplane going over. Start again. Drag the guy in …'

'I get it.'

'And that was only with a hundred of us. Can you imagine what it'll be like tomorrow with all two thousand? Chaos. Just chaos.'

You could tell from all the almost 'f' words that I was frustrated and needed calming down.

'Cup of tea?' Arny asked.

'Lipton?'

'Cat's whiskers herbal grass.'

'Sounds like shit.'

'It's local. They gave it to me in the restaurant. It's good for kidney stones.'

'What if I don't want kidney stones?'

'You're a funny girl. Too bad this movie's not a comedy.'

He eased himself onto his side and poured two glasses of cat's whiskers.

'You get fired yet?' I asked.

'No, I made it through the first day. Our hero didn't show up till early evening. I had the floor till then. I'd heard he was having a breakfast dispute but it turned out he was waiting for his A/C Sensuround, GPS-equipped trailer to arrive from Bangkok.'

'Must be tough out here in the tropics for a pansy,' I said. 'You seen Bunny Savage yet?'

He blushed hibiscus red.

'Better than that, Jimm,' he said.

'What's better than …? You talked to her?'

'I held her in my arms for an hour.'

'Yeah, then you woke up.'

'I'm serious.'

'You eaten yet?'

'Jimm, I'm serious.'

'Me too,' I said. 'Is the kitchen still open? I've had nothing but a plate of *papier mache* pork and rice since breakfast. Why are you on the floor, anyway? Don't tell me. From carrying Bunny Savage off into the sunset, right?'

'It was late afternoon but, yeah.'

'Want me to get you something to eat?'

'I stopped off for muscle relaxants and pain killers on my way back. I got something to eat then. I should be okay in the morning. Thanks for asking.'

'Guys in your fragile condition shouldn't go carrying that big imagination around.'

He looked offended.

Sissy arrived wheeling a for-hire bicycle. He parked it against the railing.

'Did you get a chance to call Bangkok?' I asked.

'Yup. Made a couple of calls from the pharmacy. I got through to director Boon's production company. They're all still in shock about his death. I talked to his personal assistant. Asked about Khin.'

'Her study grant?'

'It's frozen. They said they had no notification from Boon telling them to issue a cheque. There were three directors heading the company. The other two have promised to honour any contracts or commitments made by Boon but they had nothing on paper about our Burmese. They said there's nothing they can do.'

'Good of 'em.'

'She'll have to make do with the advance he gave her before he died.'

'She's survived on less,' I said.

'I got chatting to the secretary,' said Sissy as he chained the bike to a tree. 'I asked if she could think of anybody who'd want to kill her boss. She seems to think everyone was really fond of him. He wasn't the type to get into shady business deals. He put all his effort into making movies and left the administration decisions to the senior partner.'

'Dead end!'

'Maybe not. I asked her about Boon's next project. Get this. He was due to work here for the duration of Siam in a sort of technical advisor role. Then he'd be staying on in Fang with his crew to make a local historical drama right out there on the Siam set.'

'So,' I said, 'Boon makes a deal with the Americans to use their sets, maybe hang on to some of the extras. He saves a heap of money and the Americans don't have to worry about pulling down the wall and the palace.'

'That's how I see it.'

'Everyone's happy. So, why kill him?'

'That's where we find ourselves, my sister. The *why*.'

He walked up onto the balcony and flopped onto a recliner. Arny dragged himself into a position where he could prop his head up on the wooden balustrade.

'I got the number of Star Casting and Locations from Lizzie, OB's gofer,' said Sissy. 'Now, you'd think, given that they're coordinating for a big budget Hollywood movie, Star Casting would want to keep their finger on the pulse and make sure nothing got screwed up. You'd think they'd have a publicist there just to handle enquiries about the movie. You'd think if someone from the New York Times called them and started asking questions, they'd be only too pleased to boast about their service.'

'You told them you were New York Times?'

'I may have intimated, yeah. But you know what they did? They said all the details for the Siam project were being handled by some outsourcing company in the north. The people in Bangkok couldn't tell me a damn thing.'

I was shocked.

'They outsource for one of the biggest productions of the year?' I said.

'Exactly.'

'They give you a number for the other company?'

'Yup.'

'Fang?'

'Can't tell. They said it was in Chiang Mai, but don't go looking for a multi-story office building downtown. It's a cell phone number.'

'Damn. They don't even have a landline? They got a name?'

'The receptionist called it Northern Thai Castings.'

'Otherwise known as a guy with a cell phone. Did you call?'

'Nobody's answering.'

'Wow.' I got to my feet and stretched.

'I have to consider all the implications of this in the bathroom.' I said.

'Hurry back,' said Sissy.

I walked off the deck, the boards bouncing under my feet. I hoped it had nothing to do with the two kilos I'd packed on since starting the project. Arny winced as the floorboards rearranged themselves beneath him. He worked himself into a position where he could drink his tea. It was cold now but he couldn't reach the thermos. He looked like a seal with no hope of standing on his hind flippers for the foreseeable future. Doomed to drag himself ...

'You didn't tell me this was an actual tea party,' came a voice from the shadows.

Sissy and Arny looked up to see a sight barely more credible than an American frontiersman in Siam in 1560. Leaning on the corner beam of the cabin in comfortable jeans and a Singha Beer T-shirt was the hottest thing to hit Hollywood since the bushfires of 62.

'Oh,' they said.

'I'm fine, thanks,' she replied.

'We weren't exactly expecting you to come,' said Sissy.

'I'm not leaving,' she laughed.

'No. That's good,' said Arny attempting to climb up the railing. 'We don't want you to.'

Sissy was surprised to see his brother flustered in the company of a beautiful woman. He watched him blush and act as if the pain in his back were nothing. The boy had a crush.

'Wow,' said Sissy. 'This is like when you write a letter to the President and as a postscript you say, if you're ever passing North Pole, Idaho I'd be mighty pleased if you'd drop by, but deep down you know it isn't going to happen.'

'There's no such place as North Pole, Idaho,' she said.

'Is too.'

'I'm still not leaving.'

'Good,' said Arny, leaning now against the railing like the last drunk in the bar.

'What were you doing on the floor, Arny?' she asked.

'Yoga,' he replied.

At this stage in the performance I re-emerged onto the deck after a torrid time in the toilet, not suspecting there might be a movie star lurking in the shadows.

'I don't know,' I said. For some reason I was in my New York mode. 'I'm shitting like a rabbit these days. It's coming out in pellets. I've got to start eating better.'

'Hey, Jimm,' Sissy yelled.

'Yuh?'

'Guess who's out here on the balcony.'

'Osamah Bong Label.' I guessed.

'Good try. It's Bunny Savage.'

'Yeah?' said I, 'She here for hair and makeup tips from the country's number one grooming guru? You do realize how plain she is under all that foundation.'

I looked up at the summit of the mountain, black against a dark grey sky. The moon was somewhere up there still cloaked in its gauze of smog. I didn't even bother to look off into the bushes where my brothers were pointing. I'd fallen for that trick too many times. It was a ridiculous moment but a great one. I loved weird scenes like that. I sat in the recliner just as Bunny climbed the steps to the balcony. I was too shocked to scream but I laughed so hard my stomach ached. I knew from experience that things could only go downhill from there so I just wanted to savour the moment. I didn't even bother to apologize.

'What's so funny, girl?' Sissy asked. 'You've just offended a diva. Shame on you.'

But Bunny was impressively cool. She put her hands together in a well-constructed *wai* leaving us no choice but to return the greeting. Ours were clumsy and amateur by comparison.

Arny recovered his own cool long enough to manage an introduction.

'My sister, Jimm Juree – Ms. Bunny Savage.'

'Pleased to meet you, Jimm,' she said.

'You'd better sit down,' Sissy told her. 'Jimm's intimidated by women taller than her.'

'Which is most of the population,' I said.

The rattan chair let out its trademark creak as the actress sat but she trusted it. She looked up at the looming cliff and took a deep breath, filling her lungs with the scents of the night.

'Nice spot,' she said then looked at Arny. 'You don't look so good.'

'His back's out,' I said.

'Oh, no. It wasn't from today's scene?' she asked.

Arny was about to deny she had any culpability but Sissy didn't give him a chance.

'He had a disc out a few months back. He isn't supposed to do anything too strenuous, but you know what these career weightlifters are like. Think they're always in their teens.'

'I'm really sorry,' she said.

'Not your fault,' said Arny. 'How did you get here?

'Legs.'

'Shouldn't you be going around with a minder or something?' Sissy asked.

'Gus,' she said. 'Ex-marine. The only Jewish bodyguard in Hollywood who still wears his kippha.'

'Where is he?' I asked.

'Sitting outside my room at the Chalet. I climbed out the window.'

'What floor are you on?' asked Arny.

'Second. It was okay. The balconies are close together and there was a tree. Piece of cake.'

Sissy and I were dining out on the weirdness of it all. Arny was clearly traumatized.

'It's just like *Notting Hill*,' said Sissy, feeling certain Bunny would share his love of chick-flicks.

'The movie, not the place,' I added.

'I've seen it,' said Bunny.

Sissy floated over to the rail and sat looking at his movie star guest.

'I've dreamed this,' he said, 'in a vision. I'm Hugh Grant except I'm better looking. She meets him, just like this, by accident. She pretends not to be interested in him ...'

'She's really not pretending,' I told him.

'But she realizes she wants a simple guy like him. How sweet, how funny is this simple guy. Perhaps a little effeminate but, hell, who cares? It works for Hugh. She decides that Hollywood's too rough for a girl like her, too bullshit. And she gets it in her head to run away from it all – with him. And here she is and here he is. It's just like I saw it in my fantasy.'

'Except in your fantasy you had the Julia Roberts role,' I reminded him in Thai.

'Gee!' was all Bunny could manage.

It was a while before the laughter died down and a calm descended on the balcony.

'Man, I needed that,' Bunny told them. 'Just an honest to goodness chuckle.'

'Want some tea to go with it?' I asked.

'Sure.'

Arny lowered himself to the small table to prepare it for her. He walked to her on his knees with her tea held in front of him as would an indentured slave. She took it and dismissed him with a wave of her royal hand. I got the feeling she could have been good at a lot of things if the signs had been right; a tank commander in Iraq or a nun, or a nuclear physicist. She was ballsy. I watched her chest heave. Okay, perhaps she couldn't be a nun.

'Where are you from?' I asked.

'Boston,' she said. 'Catholic school. Nothing to do with religion.'

'How'd you get into movies,' Sissy asked.

'Hmm,' she said, 'I thought I'd be getting into teaching but I got waylaid. I'd done drama in high school, and some kid's father was a producer. He came to watch his daughter but when he got home the only close-ups on his Handi-cam were of me. He fast-tracked me through TV then onto B movies. Next thing you know I'm in Thailand with an arrow in my gut.'

I understood. Like me she was a victim of her looks. Whereas mine excluded me from the glamour careers, hers funnelled her into them. Nobody would let her teach school or drive a bus. Somewhere along the line she'd have been bullied into image servitude. There was too much money to be made out of her. She'd always be under pressure to sell herself one way or another. Yet here she was, five thousand dollars an hour, yakking with three worthless slobs. I considered that very cool.

When Sissy went to get himself some food she went with him and came back with her own plate of spicy salad and six large bottles of icy cold Leo Beer. She drank hers from the bottle.

'What about your figure?' Sissy asked.

'You kidding?' She swigged her beer. 'Ten minutes out in that heat tomorrow and this little fellow will be evaporated up into the heavens. Beers just brown water, you know?'

'Cheers to that,' said Sissy and raised his bottle.

'Which reminds me,' I said. 'You don't think Gus the bouncer's going to find us and beat the shit out of us?'

'He's not that type of body guard,' she said. 'He's mainly there to keep the paparazzi off my back and make sure nobody pokes an autograph pencil in my eye. He isn't my brother. Besides, he thinks I'm in bed.'

'How do you know there isn't a photographer over there on the far bank with a telephoto lens this minute?' Sissy asked.

'What if there is? I'm dressed and we aren't doing anything untoward. What trouble could I get in with such a harmless group?'

'She's sprung us, Jimm,' Sissy shook his head. 'She knows we're pussy cats.'

We were interrupted by a sudden commotion from behind the cabin. It was some kind of linguistic duel – English versus Thai. Neither combatant seemed prepared to yield.

'I tell you, madam, I am a guest here.' (English)

'Who the hell are you? I don't know you?' (Thai)

'If you'd just allow me to knock on one or two more doors I'm sure …' (English)

'You're annoying my guests, darkie. Get your skinny lizard ass out of my resort (Thai)

I rushed out to intervene. I'd recognized the intruder's voice and knew right away the poor woman was no match for the burly manageress of the resort. After a few minutes of platitudes and pleadings, I returned to the balcony with Khin under my wing.

'She ... she actually had a knife,' the Burmese said. 'You don't suppose she ...?'

'She would have gutted you in a heartbeat,' Sissy told her. 'How you doing, you night stalker?'

'Rather grateful to be alive, it would seem,' said Khin. 'Ah, we have a daughter of Eve in our midst.'

'Khin Thein Aye,' said Sissy. 'This is *the* Bunny Savage.'

Khin shook her hand and said, 'Pleased to make your acquaintance.'

'And yours,' she replied.

'You're a very attractive young lady. Are you married?'

Cinema fanzines were apparently not on Khin's reading list.

'Happily. Three bonny children,' Bunny replied.

'That's nice. Anyway,' Khin addressed the balcony, 'I have excellent news. I have translated a very important manuscript in Pa Sang.'

'Well done,' said Sissy. 'What's it say?'

'Wait,' said Arny making the appropriate hand signal. 'We have to call a time-out here.' The tweaked nerve had been temporarily subdued by the beer and the painkillers and he was vertical again. 'We have a guest. It's only fair that we tell her about Khin.'

Sissy and I were able to summarize the entire nutty Khin story in three minutes. We told it like a pirate booty hunt and left Bunny in no doubt that poor Khin was hanging onto sanity by a thread. Only Khin seemed to miss the sarcastic tone.

'Okay, Khin,' said Arny. 'You're on.'

'And not a moment too soon,' said Khin, managing to lower herself onto the same recliner as me. It let out a plea for mercy but held us both.

'Brothers Sissy and Arny,' she began, 'Sister Jimm and new Sister Bunny, I have made a remarkable discovery.'

'You found the treasure?' I asked.

'Not quite,' she said. 'It transpires that I have been flogging a dead horse.'

'Meaning, no, right?' I asked Bunny.

'Yes.'

'There's no treasure?' said Arny.

'That isn't what I'm saying,' said Khin. 'My discovery is that the treasure I have been seeking may very well be a myth.'

'Alleluia,' I said. 'Khin's come home to us.'

'Welcome back to our planet,' said Sissy.

'I feel like I'm at a reunion of the Stooges,' said Bunny. 'You guys should go on the road with this.'

'So, Khin,' Sissy shook his head, 'if the treasure's a myth, why are you looking so pleased with yourself?'

'Because I was extremely clever to be able to uncover my misapprehension,' said Khin.

I turned to Bunny. 'She's a classic.'

'There is, true enough, something classical about me,' Khin confirmed. 'Perhaps if you'd share with me a little marijuana I might be able to convince you of my dexterity.'

We all looked guiltily at Bunny.

'Don't mind me, guys,' she said. 'I've got beer.'

So I retrieved our stash from the secret compartment in the jeep, and expertly rolled a joint in the front seat where the paparazzi wouldn't see me. Khin filled in the wait by asking Bunny what she did for a living and rechecking that she was spoken for. When I returned, Khin allowed the good Burmese weed to creep along her inner passages before resuming the story.

'You may recall,' she began, 'my original theory being that the first king of the Mangrai dynasty ...'

'King Mangrai,' Sissy interrupted.

'Thank you, Sissy,' said Khin. 'Yes, that Mangrai himself had buried the Ngoen Yang regalia and the coronation jewels in respect for his ancestors. But, that twenty-eight kings later, King Kawila had somehow found the loot and used it during his own coronation. Fearing that he had offended the spirits he ordered the treasure reburied. It has been in search of this latter interment that I have been investing my efforts.'

She took another drag.

A natural quartet of 'But?'

'But' she said, 'I found two independent descriptions of Kawila's coronation in the chronicles. One was in ancient Mon, a script with which I have some familiarity. It goes into great detail.'

She reached into her back pack and removed a dog-eared wad of folded papers. She slowly started to shuffle her way through them.

'You can see why we don't need a TV,' Sissy said to Bunny.

'She's climbing my chart of favourite living characters,' she smiled.

'What makes you think she's alive?' I asked.

Khin was by now impervious to extraneous comments. An historian with a Mon transcription was like an alcoholic with a fresh fourth of gin. 'If I may read you my actual translation,' she continued, 'and please excuse my poor rendition. It says, "And Kawila was splendidly regaled. Like Mangrai so many years before him he held aloft the semblance of the Sikanchai dagger whose blade glinted proudly in the sunlight."'

The audience waited patiently for her to continue, for some kind of punch line, but Khin merely grinned at them, looking from face to face in the dim moonlight.

'That's it?' I asked.

'Yes.'

'That's the line that killed off your treasure hunt?'

'In its original form, most certainly,' she agreed.

'Why?' Bunny asked.

'Well, he says it, doesn't he?' said Khin, '"The semblance of the Sikanchai dagger". It obviously wasn't the real thing. Kawila made copies of the royal regalia based on the historical records at his disposal.'

'Whoa, girl,' I reined her in. 'You're saying the entire destruction of your theory comes down to the word, 'semblance'? A word that you translated yourself from an ancient Mon text? You sure you couldn't have – oh, I don't know – screwed up on the translation a little bit?'

Others would certainly have been offended, but not Khin.

'Yes, I'm sure,' she said.

'How can you be?' Bunny asked.

'The writer was an eye witness,' said Khin, 'or at the very least, he got his account from an eye witness.'

'You guess,' I said.

'I'm confident.'

'Even so,' said Sissy, 'it's a sad death for an otherwise good theory based on that one word.'

'But, my pet, don't you see?' said Khin. 'He confirms it.'

'How so?'

'In the line, "Its blade glinted proudly in the sunlight".'

'Now, you're not about to argue it was overcast that day?' I said.

'Better than that,' said Khin. 'The Sikanchai was an ancient ceremonial dagger. It dated back to before the eleventh century. It was cast in simple kilns from local material. It was made of dull iron – probably black. There was no glinting to be had.'

A hush descended upon the group as the mental penny dropped. We all found ourselves nodding slowly.

'This is better than *The West Wing*,' Bunny clapped her hands, glee plastered all over her face.

'So, it's all over,' I said. 'The Kawila guy was a con man. Let's call the time police, have him picked up.'

'Oh, Jimm,' Khin beamed. 'It isn't all over in the least. Don't you see? It's just the beginning. Kawila didn't discover Mangrai's treasure.'

'So?'

'Mangrai's treasure is exactly where he buried it.'

'And that is?'

'... the next excruciating episode of "Khin's adventures in The Land Without a Clue",' said Sissy.

'I confess I may have to go back over some notes,' said Khin, 'but this narrows down the field remarkably. I'm so excited about it I have to take a shower. If you'll excuse me.' She rose awkwardly from our seat. 'Where am I sleeping tonight?'

She went inside without waiting for an answer. Bunny watched until we heard the bathroom door slam shut.

'She's something else.'

'She sure is,' Sissy agreed.

'Do you think she really believes it all?' asked Bunny. 'The treasure?'

I looked at Sissy before answering. When I spoke it was with my voice lowered.

'Khin's a smart lady,' I said. 'If she lived anywhere else in the world but Burma she'd be earning a fortune as head of department at some fancy university. She's fluent in languages that died long before Fred Flintstone learned to drive. But she's from over there in Burma, and to tell the truth they've got nothing much to look forward to or believe in right now. Khin had the balls to bail out. She's living in a foreign country. If this treasure fantasy gives her just a little bit of pleasure – something to dream of - I'm all for it.'

'Me too,' said Sissy.

'Me too,' said Arny.

'Me too,' said Bunny.

The lights over the distant bridge briefly reflected in a tiny tear at the top of her cheek.

'Look guys,' she said, 'this has been an evening I won't forget in a while but I've got lines to learn before tomorrow. I'm off.'

'I'll walk you back,' Arny said. He'd spent much of the past half hour staring at the starlet. I wondered whether my brother had fallen in love for the first time.

'No you won't,' she said. 'You'll take another two muscle pills and get back down there on the deck.

You've got to be in shape for tomorrow. I've checked the script. You get to carry my wounded horse.'

'Really?' said Arny.

'No,' she replied. 'But you do need a rest.'

'Then I insist on sending my trusted man-servant, Sissy,' I said. My brother leapt to his feet and bowed.

'It's only five hundred yards,' she pleaded.

'The French were defeated at Dien Piang Phu in five hundred yards,' Sissy told her and left her with no choice.

'Then … see you,' she said.

'Night,' we replied.

'I'm really sorry about your back,' she said to Arny and bent down to give him a kiss on the cheek.

'Not a problem,' he lied, burning red.

'Say 'bye' to Khin for me,' said Bunny.

'Will do.'

She looked back briefly before disappearing behind the cabin. It was a look that carried some warmth. The voices faded into the night and there was just me on my recliner, Arny supine on the balcony and the sound of Khin cleaning her teeth with my brush.

Chapter 9

"Good morning, and in case I don't see ya, good afternoon, good evening, and good night!"
The Truman Show (1998)

It was sometime before dawn when I heard Arny's voice in the darkness.

'Jimm? You awake?'

'Yeah.'

'Jimm, do you think she likes me?'

'Everybody likes you, Arny,' I said. 'Look at you. You're gorgeous. Why else would she be here? You really did get to carry her to bed on film. I'm seriously impressed. How's your back?'

Arny was lying on the floor between the twin beds. Khin had commandeered one. She was snoring rudely. Sissy was in the hammock on the balcony. The pre-dawn cocks were rehearsing.

'It's hard to tell,' said Arny. 'You spend the night on wood and you're going to be pretty sore anyway. You've just got to distinguish which is the floor agony and which is the post-op agony.'

'You know what you need?' I asked.

'Traction?'

'A swim in the river.'

It wasn't a logical idea but it sounded oddly appealing.

'The sun's not up yet,' he said.

'Does that stop the river being cool and wet? And we aren't going back to sleep with her grunting over there.'

I threw my pillow at the noisemaker. Khin awoke, not like a woman assaulted by kapok but like a genius who'd just had a profound idea. There may have been a little light bulb in the air above her head.

'Hey, Khin,' I said, 'wanna go for a swim?'

'I'd be tickled pink,' she said, drowsily.

'That's "yes" right?'

Five minutes later, the amok runners – Sissy included – in nothing but our underwear were mid-stream in front of the cabin watching the sun peer over the mountain. The pull of the current was like an early massage. The tour boats began their journey beyond the bridge downstream so we didn't have to swim in diesel and chip packets. The water carried a clean chill from the hills and we felt the way Mangrai's men must have felt five centuries earlier. If we stood facing south west and looked at the tree-covered slopes, the buildings and the overhead cables and riverside beer garden at our backs, this was exactly the view the king would have enjoyed. I imagined him standing in that same mud washing away the dust and blood of battle. For a while I felt that same electric surge of history that had probably flowed through Khin's blood since she was a young nerd at home in Yangon.

After a brief playful attempt to drown Khin we grabbed her arms and waded her back toward the hut. The sun fought its way through the haze and bathed the rooftops in a dingy orange. We felt invigorated, ready for a new day.

Then a bang.

Then a thump.

It was the first thing I felt, like being slapped by a wall of air. It whipped all four of us back into the water. I floundered beneath the surface, disoriented. It was one of the first times I thought I might be about to die. Shock. Panic. Confusion. What in hell? I righted myself and found my feet. Before me the cabin blazed like a July fourth bonfire. I looked behind me. Khin and my brothers stood to their waists in the silver red water, the light from the flames dancing on their skins.

Chapter 10

"I love the smell of napalm in the morning."
Apocalypse Now. (1979)

The first official police appraisal was that the LP gas tank had been faulty. Each cabin had an eleven-kilogram tank at its rear connected to the shower.

'This is Thailand', the officer reminded them, as if that explained away all unnatural disasters. 'The things are notoriously unstable. They blow up all the time. It's impossible to regulate all the dealers,' etcetera.

The resort owner, still in her bright red Chinese pyjamas, had apologized a thousand times to her damp and shaken guests. She brought us unfashionable tracksuits from her husband's closet and held her hands together permanently, in deference to the money she'd lose if the movie people cancelled. She envisaged her windfall being swept away in a gas tank panic. She personally went from room to room disconnecting the hoses.

It had been circumspect to have Khin removed from the premises before the police turned up. She'd taken herself to the far bank of the river where she hid wrapped in a black plastic garbage bag. Of course she hadn't been able to dress first as her clothes had been consumed in the fire along with our bags and money and reading material and toiletries. From our vantage point in the bungalow restaurant we could see Khin's feet protruding from behind a bush. We hoped she wouldn't catch pneumonia.

The lone policeman had returned to the kiosk to write up his report. The grips and best boys and extras billeted at the Garden Home had caught the seven o'clock movie bus to the location so word of the "accident" soon made its way around the set. The owner was off in search of alternative accommodation for her almost-blown-to-kingdom-come guests. The gardeners were all very respectful of the guests whose karma had put them out of harm's way. They came by to squeeze the shoulders of the survivors in hope that some of the good fortune might rub off on them.

When all was quiet I whistled for Khin to join us. She was an elegant swimmer and a gaunt practitioner of the breast stroke. We requisitioned a large towel from the housekeeper and wrapped the Burmese in it. Alone with the canteen staff and large mugs of sweet instant coffee we were pensive. It was some time before we could think of anything to say. Four heaped plates of fried rice had appeared in front of us on the small metal card table but we looked at them benumbed.

'It was an accident,' Khin said hopefully.

We nodded.

'These things blow up all the time.'

We heard a car approaching along the narrow resort pathways. It was a gold SUV with ominous tinted windows and a Thai flag jutting ambassadorially from the fender. It passed us, went as far as the burnt-out cabin then reversed to the restaurant. After a moment of apparent contemplation the passenger door opened and out stepped a uniformed police major. He was perhaps forty and the decorations on his dress shirt suggested he'd won several wars single-handedly. He was tall and thin but his face was wide as if it had been shut in a sandwich press and his features had spread. His hair was military short but receding to a tongue of bristles at the forehead. From the other door stepped a policeman with a camera hanging from his shoulder and a small tape recorder in one hand.

The major approached our table and eyed the four inhabitants. Khin twitched but I gestured for her to calm down. The officer's eyes settled on Sissy.

'You're the ones who escaped the explosion?' he asked. His voice was husky as if the northern fog had settled in his throat. He spoke unnecessarily loudly suggesting he wanted the staff to hear. Sissy nodded. He wasn't particularly fond of police. The cameraman snapped our picture. The officer stood erect. His long arms ended in fists. He looked at the four of us, one at a time as if committing our faces to memory.

'I am Major Ketthai of the Fang central command,' he said. 'I am very sorry to hear of your inconvenience. We will naturally contact the company that manufactures these tanks and investigate their safety standards. This is a peaceful place but I imagine you'll want to be returning to where you came from after such an upsetting circumstance. Disasters have a nasty habit of coming in pairs, don't you find?'

He waited, perhaps for a respectful *wai* from our group at the table but when none was forthcoming he glared, turned on his heel and waved the cameraman back into the car. He in turn climbed into the back seat and slammed the door. The SUV did a three-point-turn and kicked up gravel as it departed.

We watched it go.

'Were we just threatened?' Sissy asked.

'I guess,' said I.

We translated the scene for Khin who seemed to miss the underlying menace.

'Well, that was certainly very civilized of him to come all this way to see if we were well,' she said.

'Khin!' My pitch often climbed when Khin failed to grasp important points. 'He wasn't here on a courtesy visit.'

'Jimm,' she said, 'you do have a habit of building dungeons in the air.'

I had no idea what that meant.

'Maybe,' said Sissy, 'but you just met the keeper of the keys.'

'How so?'

'We just had a visit from a police major,' I told her. 'He's based in Fang which is about twenty-five minutes away. But, it's only seven thirty, still half an hour from office hours. So, they'd have to pull the good major out of his bed, get him dressed and drive at full throttle to have him here at this time. Given that our local cop didn't get here till 6:40 and he didn't call anyone while he was investigating, I'd say the major wasn't informed of our little accident by anybody until he was on his way here.'

'But, that means ...' Khin pondered.

'It means he knew it was going to happen,' I said.

'And, he didn't bring the camera guy for a team picture of the survivors,' Sissy added. 'They came all this way to investigate a death. They wanted pictures of the bodies.'

'Oh, I say,' said Khin.

'For some reason remaining to be seen,' I said, 'we've upset someone on the police force and we've just had our first and second warnings.'

We continued to sit and drink coffee and shake our heads a lot until the sound of a second expensive engine edged its way through the narrow lanes towards us. It was a Lexus GX Utility and it rolled sedately up to the restaurant steps like a lava flow. We feared the worst but when the door opened it was Lizzie, OB's gofer, who stepped out. She was a short, wild-haired girl of an unguessable age. She jogged over to us with a concerned furrow to her brow.

'Oh, guys,' she said. She hugged us in turn, even Khin, whom she'd never met. 'We were so worried about you. We heard what happened. We've all been praying for your safety. Are you okay?'

'Shouldn't you be directing a guy directing a movie?' Sissy asked.

'The world stops when one of our boys goes down. Leave no man behind. Life, what can I say? It's so precious.'

I began to understand where all the old clichés went to die.

'Well, thanks for dropping by,' I said.

'You may think there's nothing to live for now but there's always a silver lining,' she said. 'Here!'

She put a large fat envelope on the table in front of us. We could all smell money.

'It's from the contingency fund,' she said. 'I know it can't begin to replace those personal effects and treasures that were taken from you but it should help you get back on your feet till payday.'

'Gee, thanks,' I said. I had no intention of doing the, "We couldn't possibly accept this," routine.

'The boss says he doesn't need you to come in today,' she said.

'You're going to need a new frontiersman shirt,' I told her. 'The last one's kind of melted.'

'Don't you worry your sweet head about anything,' said Lizzie. 'It's all taken care of. Gotta go.'

She skipped back to the idling vehicle and was gone. I flipped open the top of the envelope to see a very healthy wad of dollars.

'Shit,' said Arny, 'we should get blown up more often.'

'Only thing I lost of value was my dear departed's roach clip,' Sissy said. 'You lose anything of value, Jimm?'

'My cell phone,' I said. 'A good pair of Nikes.'

'You, Khin?'

'Several pages of notes,' she said. 'But most of it is etched on my mind. Oh, and a rather splendid handmade skirt.'

'They exploded your skirt, Khin?' Sissy smiled. 'And you said those things were best Burmese quality.'

'Yes,' she said. 'Regrettably not bomb-proof. Do we actually have any evidence that the explosion was not an accident?'

'You ever seen a gas container explode, Khin?' I asked.

'Not as such. I have heard one or two.'

'Well, the two usual causes are a faulty valve or exposure to intense heat. Most gas containers explode when there's a fire in a kitchen and the bottle ruptures. You might get a crack in an old bottle and the leak's exposed to a spark or a naked flame. Either way, the gas explodes and bursts the container like a Coke tin. There'd be a flash of fire but not enough to engulf our little cabin in flames in two seconds. That would take something containing petroleum or a liquid explosive. You see that hole over there, Khin?'

She turned in her seat to see a hole the size of a bin lid in the side of the wooden restaurant store area. The staff were putting a temporary plywood band aid on it.

'Heavens,' said Khin.

'While we were waiting for the country's finest to arrive, Sissy and I did a little bit of investigating of our own. My trusty police dog Sissy climbed in through the restaurant hole and came out with this.'

Sissy lifted himself from the seat and pulled out a pancake-shaped version of the gas bottle. He'd been using it as a cushion till the fuss died down.

'You see,' I said, 'gas containers don't implode, they explode like balloons. What this tells us is that whatever made the bang was beside the LP bottle, not inside it.'

'Then why are you concealing the evidence under your bottom?' she asked.

'You want us to hand it over to the cops?' Sissy asked. 'We don't know what we've done wrong yet so we don't know who the good guys are.'

Khin took a sip of her cold coffee until a thoroughly guilty look appeared on her face.

'You don't suppose they were after the treasure, do you?'

We laughed which left our Burmese friend confused.

'Khin,' I said. 'There is no treasure. I mean, not yet anyway. Until you dig the stuff up there is no point in killing you. Know what I mean?'

'Plus they had no way of knowing you'd be turning up here last night,' Sissy pointed out. 'No, for whatever reason, me and Jimm and Arny are somebody's enemies.'

'Then what in the devil's name are you going to do about it?' asked Khin.

I watched a gang of hill tribe girls gathering at the river's edge, preparing for their daily assault on tourists. They were decorating one another with their silver finery and practicing their unrelenting hard sell patter out loud.

'You don't mind walking around Fang in a bath towel, do you?' I asked.

'Certainly not,' she said. 'It's rather like a *longyi*. They'll just assume I'm another eccentric Burmese.'

Our Suzuki had been parked at the end of the row of cabins. As the main keys were molten and speeding through outer space somewhere we retrieved the spares from under the rubber mat and headed out of the bungalow complex.

'One final question,' Khin said, turning to me in the back seat.

'Oh, I doubt that but go ahead,' I said.

'How, may I ask, did you get to be so *au fait* with the workings and aerodynamics of the common gas bottle?'

'Camping,' I said. 'I was in the girl guides.'

'I see.'

For some mysterious reason that answer seemed to satisfy her.

There wasn't a pair of slacks in the whole of Fang that could cover the distance from Khin's waist to her ankles. Everything stopped mid-shin and made her look retarded. Her size thirteen feet were horrors they only read about in shoe shop science fiction comics. So Khin had no choice but to buy her travelling wardrobe at the Fang Sporting Goods Emporium – man section. She and Sissy settled on two pairs of shorts apiece and two European soccer club shirts. We all selected from the range of jogging footwear and Arny just squeezed into the largest size of lilac polo shirt in the store and silver cross-trainers with luminous heels. As they didn't cater for pelicans, Khin resorted to flip flops that left her heels dragging. As for me I went Wimbledon tennis, all white with a visor.

We bought genuine Abibas day packs, faked right there at the store, and replaced toiletries and underwear. 1 rummaged around for reading material and came back with magazines and an illustrated Fang history.

To round off the morning we sat down to a sumptuous meal at the finest restaurant in Fang, wryly named the Fang Restaurant. It was all that remained of the old Fang Hotel which stood empty and sad next door. We looked out on the busy street. It was as if all the people milling around the town were visitors intent on doing their business and getting away. Nobody seemed to idle or loiter there. Cars stopped in front of stores with their engines running while the drivers hurried to pick things up or drop things off.

Despite our reckless spending spree the amok runners had taken only a very small bite from the discretionary fund handout. I calculated that the remainder would be enough to feed an underprivileged hill tribe village for several months. We toyed with the idea of making such a donation but soon got over it and divvied it up between the four of us. Ignoring her protestations, we drove Khin to the bus station and bought her a ticket back to Chiang Mai.

'I think it would be a jolly good idea if you all forgot this cinema idea and returned also,' she said.

'Come on, Khin,' I said. 'Things are just starting to get interesting.'

'You'd be surprised how disappointing 'interesting' can look from the inside of a coffin, Sister Jimm,' she said. 'Somebody tried to blow you up.'

'We laugh in the face of danger,' said Sissy with little conviction.

'Mad as hatters, the pair of you.'

The Fang bus station was a gathering area for two-plank trucks, airless hire cars, and three-wheeled rickshaws. When the actual bus arrived they all yielded like courtiers from an empress. The bus stopped, the door opened, and a screaming youth in a white shirt jumped onto the platform.

'Chiang Dao. Mae Taeng, Mae Rim, Chiang Mai.'

One old lady climbed down the steps and was consumed in a feeding frenzy of porters and motorcycle taxi drivers. Once they were sure no other passengers planned to alight they slunk back to their benches and their comics and their board games. Sissy and Arny pushed Khin towards the bus.

'Get a move on, Khin,' I said. 'They only stop long enough to put down and pick up.'

'But comrades,' she said. 'I feel like this is the time that you need me most.'

The bus was rolling now, the youth running alongside attempting to coerce passengers into a journey they didn't want to make. Khin skipped onto the bottom step and left one flip flop on the concrete.

'King Mangrai needs you more,' Sissy shouted as the bus picked up speed. The youth leapt past Khin and up the steps.

'Bring home the you-know-what,' I shouted, throwing the flip flop into Khin's arms. She remained on the step, looking like a destitute footballer, until the dust and fumes turned the bus into a mucky cloud. We waved it away.

I turned to my brothers.

'You know? I wouldn't think any less of you if you followed her,' I said.

'No?' said Sissy.

'No.'

'And what would you do without us?' said Arny.

'Oh, the usual. Finish my movie. Have an affair with Dan Jensen that leaves him heartbroken and ruined. Write my article.'

'That's all?'

'Sure.'

'You wouldn't go off on some hell-fired vendetta to find out who killed director Boon and who blew up our cabin?' he asked.

'Absolutely not...well, only if I got a couple of hours off work. I don't have any choice. It's written in the crime reporter's code, "For Justice We Do the Irresponsible". So, you going home?'

Arny seemed to give it some thought but Sissy laughed off the idea.

'You ain't got wheels, man,' he said in English, 'and I don't have an income at present so I can't afford to give up this job.'

'That's my boy,' I said and kissed him on the cheek.

'I'm staying,' said Arny and I gave him a smack on the kisser too.

'Where to first?' Sissy asked.

'Fang police headquarters,' I said.

'Very funny.'

'I'm serious. I've got a protection plan worked out.'

'Oh man.'

'We might have to make a couple of stops on the way.'

Chapter 11

"I don't remember a time when I didn't want to be a police officer ... apart from the summer of 1979 when I wanted to be Kermit the Frog."
Hot Fuzz (2006)

Sgt. Chat was letting the limp hose water caress his motorcycle while he worked the sponge. Chat knew he'd have himself a truck soon enough. He'd done a few odd jobs for the major – been given little thank you gifts. Nothing substantial but a sign of trust. Yes, he'd buy a truck soon, have matching Serpico mud flaps on the rear tyres, Che Guavaras at the front. He had no idea who they were but he'd seen them on enough long distance trucks. He knew they'd protect him from the usual carnage of the road.

Chat, the desk sergeant at the Fang police headquarters, was under-worked. When they were still down in the town there used to be walk-ins. But once they moved up to that neat expensive-looking station at the end of its own paved road things slowed down a lot. People seemed to get the idea the police had more important things to do than offer public assistance. Fang folk were taking care of their own problems these days.

Chat wasn't certain what went on in the upstairs offices. There had to be cases, he guessed. The inspectors and detectives put in long hours so there had to be something going on. But if anyone did stop by to report a crime, the senior people usually let the uniforms on the ground floor handle it.

Chat wasn't an unaware man. Crime fighting had changed since he joined the force twenty years earlier. He read the newspapers. It was all white collar and computer fraud. He knew that's what they'd be doing upstairs; clandestine stuff like the body in the pond. They couldn't tell him what that was all about. He was sworn to secrecy. Ask no questions. Just do what you're told. Keep focused on the fact there has to be a bigger picture. He scratched his balls. They'd been itching for two weeks. Damn that pond.

A red Suzuki Caribbean came huffing up the dead-end drive and crunched on the gravel frontage. Chat watched from behind his motorcycle. The driver was a Thai, good looking, middle-aged guy with a chubby girl beside him. In the back sat a small mountain of a boy who filled his shirt sleeves. Beside him was a fellow he recognized called Arun and a skinny white female in a gypsy costume. Arun was the local stringer for the *Chiang Mai News*. He covered road accidents and fetes and local council meetings. He knew better than to be messing around with police business. The jeep turned around and parked under a far tree.

Chat turned off his hose, wiped his hands on a cloth, and scratched the inside of his thigh before walking over to the visitors.

'Problem?' he asked.

Chapter 12

**"I was the only guy who disagreed with the cops -
and I had brain damage."**
Memento (2000)

'Good afternoon, officer,' I said. 'We're here to see Major Ketthai.'

'Is he expecting you?' the policeman asked, looking at me suspiciously.

'He'll be pleased to see us,' I said. 'We have good news.'

The cop glared at the press guy.

'What are you doing here?' he asked.

Arun smiled and shrugged.

'Local story,' he said. 'Police doing a good job, you know?'

The cop hesitated then led us all to the front desk in the open reception area. The seats were bus terminal style, joined together with metal rods. No danger of anyone walking off with those seats. He had us sit and spoke on the phone with his hand cupping the mouthpiece.

The major was downstairs in seconds.

'What's going on?' he asked gruffly. He looked shocked when he saw us all sitting there.

'Major Ketthai,' I *wai'd* as did the others. 'It's me, from this morning.'

'And?'

'Well,' I continued, 'as you know, they're making a movie up here. The director was so happy with your personal involvement in our little accident that he contacted the US embassy. He gave them your name and suggested they commend you to the police ministry. They agreed it would be good publicity for the movie and excellent for your career. They'd like a picture and a few words – Thai/US ties, working together in the field – that type of thing. They'll send it to *The Nation* and the *Post*. This is Margaret from Reuters. She'll get the story out through the wire services.'

'Hi,' said Margaret.

'Arun here will make sure it gets into the local paper and we're sure the national Thai press will pick it up. Public interest story. Everyone loves them.'

The concrete expression on the major's face reluctantly cracked a smile.

'Very well, but make it fast. I'm busy.'

The photo belied his ambivalence. He put his arm around the survivors' shoulders and found a fatherly smile from somewhere deep. The reporters interviewed him with me translating for Margaret and the deed was done. We dropped off Arun who promised they'd have the story in the following day's paper. The movie was big news in otherwise silent Fang, and Chiang Mai was looking for as many *Siam* related articles as they could get. Margaret, we returned to the Wieng Kaew Hotel where we'd found her. She was a backpacker, game for anything. She had no connection to Reuters or any other agency but she had a nice camera and now, several interesting Thai pictures for her album.

When we were alone, my siblings and I drove back in the direction of Tha Ton.

'You think it worked?' I asked.

'We caught him by surprise,' said Sissy. 'If he'd had time to think about it I doubt he'd have agreed. I'd say by now he's worked out what a mistake it all was. At least we're not nobodies anymore. He'll think twice about disappearing us.'

'If he buys it,' said Arny.

'It's just injected that element of doubt,' I told him. 'We might be full of shit but we might just know important people, too. Attack is the best form of defence.'

'I bet someone famous said that,' said Arny.

'I bet.'

Chapter 13

"... they may take our lives, but they'll never take our FREEDOM!"
Braveheart (1995)

Karma picked up for a while. The landlady at Garden Home found us a house. It had been built by an elderly Swiss accountant. He'd had a fatal heart attack on top of his young Thai bride and didn't really get to appreciate the place. As there were major obstacles in foreigners owning property, the house and land were in his wife's name. She needed an income more than she needed a luxurious two-story villa on the river with a mountain panorama. Her agent hadn't found a buyer at the exorbitant price she was asking so, while she was off hunting for a new husband, she left the keys with an acquaintance who happened to be related to the Garden Home manager.

The building was basically a wooden chalet - a tropical ski lodge. There was nothing Thai about it apart from the spirit house that stood inside the main gate devoid of offerings. The resident land spirits would be hungry – and probably mean. The gate itself was further evidence that money didn't buy taste. It was an ornate metal web of tridents and artful spears. The landlady handed me the keys and told me she would charge no more than the cost of our previous cabin. She was doing all she could to keep the film people happy and her bungalows full. We stood at the front door shaking our heads.

'Wow!' Arny's favourite word.

'I guess it'll do,' Sissy agreed.

It was a little bare of decorations inside, evidently due to the fact the bride had sold off most of the antiques and pictures. But there was furniture, and wood was its own decoration so it didn't feel bare. There were three bedrooms on the upper floor overlooking the river. Each bedroom had an en-suite. There was a large kitchen, an office, a living room that took up much of the ground floor and a sauna. But the piece de resistance, especially for us Jurees who did a lot of lounging and puffing, was the balcony out back. It was as wide as a badminton court and there were six teak wood recliners lined up on the deck. They were so heavy it took two of us to shift each one. Our view was all Mangrai with not a wire or a pipe or a pole in sight.

When the sun went down, Arny had an early night to rest his back. We experimented with the light switches and found one on the balcony that lit up the whole mountainside opposite. The floodlights were concealed in the lush vegetation. They were strategically placed so as to highlight, but not drown the natural flora and cast a green glow on the Kok. It turned the jungle into a mysterious place, like staring into the embers of a coal fire.

Thanks be to Buddha we had marijuana. The Fang market sold it in large plastic bags and called it vegetable. We'd bought enough to fill the secret Suzuki stash compartment and we sat on the ski-lodge deck and passed a joint the size of a small dachshund between us.

'They'd need a missile to get us now,' Sissy decided. 'But, better than that, you know what we have here, sister? We have us a party house.'

'Yeah.'

'I mean, forget assassination by the local cops. We can have some serious boogey in this place.'

We talked movies for a while and told jokes at the expense of Dan Jensen but soon the weed started to pull us backwards into a deep mire of introspection and suddenly I had nobody to talk to. I forgot Sissy was there. I felt an obligation to have serious thoughts. I considered myself. I was, what? Approaching middle-age, no children and no hope of getting any, cursed with womanhood, short-legged and smart-arsed. Two tokes later I was imagining Dan Jensen's toned muscles on top of me and I was lost.

Chapter 14

**"Your skin, your long neck. The back. The line of
you. You're why cavemen chiselled on walls."**
As Good As It Gets (1997)

The shooting location had become a planet. There was
literally a cast of thousands. Slight-bodied extras milled
around speaking in incomprehensible tongues. Arny in
his newly-sewn frontiersman coat was on a hill looking
down at them. We were astounded by the impossible
logistics of it all and the military precision it took to
create pandemonium. Three cameras on a scaffold
behind Arny worked on his back. Assistant director
Quirk now had a team of his own assistants
coordinating the crowd. Today they were despondent
city dwellers. Tomorrow they'd be courageous Thai
warriors, thence evil Burmese invaders. They didn't
have a clue or a care. They'd pick up their day wages
and return home flush and unaware of the contribution
they'd made to world cinema.

Sissy and I were taking it in turns to watch over
Arny. The head cameraman had him walk closer to the
edge of the cliff and stand on a patch of crumbling
rock. He went without a whimper and looked down
across the quarter-city and the valley beyond. I stupidly
positioned myself directly below him to break his fall. It
was probably time for us to accept the fact he wasn't
seven any more.

At one stage, I found myself sitting beside a bushy-
haired Thai who was wearing a yellow safari shirt.
Yellow was the colour of the season as the population
celebrated the sixtieth year on the throne of our

beloved king. Clothing markets overflowed with royal yellow. Some days, a stroll down a crowded main street was like wading through custard.

'Hello,' I said.

The middle-aged tired-looking man turned his head slowly toward me as if a potted plant beside him had learned to speak.

'But, your Thai is very good,' he said.

'I guess you pick it up when you use it every day for thirty three years,' I replied.

'Sorry,' he said. 'I assumed you were one of them.'

He pointed his chin towards the sea of flesh below.

'You aren't dressed for the sixteenth century,' I said. 'What do you do here?'

'I am a representative of the Ministry of Culture, he said.

'Really? I wasn't aware they let you lot leave the building. I'd heard you were all chained to your desks.'

The man laughed. 'Yes, I escaped. It's a rare privilege.'

'So, why are you here?'

'The ministry likes to have an advisor on set to point out historical or cultural errors,' he said.

'You mean things like by 1560 the Burmese had already pretty much completed their rout of Lanna?'

'Yes, things like that. And the fact that the enemy's King Maeku wasn't a fierce and great leader. In fact he was only a regent in name. He was a clerical ringer brought in by the nobles and the Burmese approved it. He had no qualifications to command an army. A couple of years later they assassinated him.'

I couldn't wait to tell Sissy.

'And you point these things out?' I said.

'Absolutely.'

'And nobody takes any notice of you.'

'The producers have more pressing concerns.'

'So, nobody in Bangkok has the balls to tell them, "If you screw up our history you can't make your movie"?'

'Young lady, ours is a money culture. There's a good deal of revenue to be had from a cinematic production. Even my own ministry gets a share.'

I admired his candor.

'Do you happen to know why they chose to film here in Fang?' I asked.

'It's historically appropriate.'

'It's the sixteenth century,' I said. 'Anywhere with trees and mountains is appropriate. It could be filmed in any one of thirty provinces.'

'That's true,' he said. 'It's usually up to the US-based producers to choose. The location company in Thailand recommends a spot and asks the province to put in a bid.'

'What kind of bid?'

'It's like a sporting event – the Asia Games, for example. They say how much it will cost to feed and accommodate X number of film people. Fang was given the contract because their bid was the lowest.'

'So the district isn't actually making a lot of money out of it?'

'Full hotel rooms, restaurants, transportation.'

'For two weeks.'

'It's a tidy sum.'

'But surely there's some kind of … I don't know … fee? Local tax? Kick back?'

'Oh, no. We would never allow it. The producers have to submit their books to the Ministry of Interior so we can check that there was no corruption at the local level. We do all we can to ensure Hollywood comes back repeatedly. We have to be certain they aren't cheated.'

'That doesn't sound very Thai,' I said.

'Oh, you'd be surprised how strict the government can be if it thinks it's being deprived of income. Look, excuse me. They appear to be flying a seventeenth century flag on the parapet again. I'd better go and say something. I'm sorry.' He stood and dusted down his pants.

'Thanks for the insight,' I said.

'You're very welcome. Your Thai is very good.' This time he meant it.

'Yours too.'

The man laughed and walked off, leaving me deep in thought on my Styrofoam rock. If corruption were the key to all this intrigue there'd have to be better takings at stake than a few plates of fried rice and a tent. Surely that couldn't be reason enough to kill a director and three nice siblings from Chiang Mai. There had to be something more.

Three hours later, I still hadn't worked out what could possess anyone to kill me. It wasn't as if Sissy or I had done anything. Sure, we'd been at the hotel the night before Boon was killed. We'd contacted Star Casting and Locations in Bangkok and failed repeatedly to get through to Northern Thai Castings. But Sissy had called from a pay phone in town so there'd be no record of his number. No way of knowing who'd called or why. No, the enemy thought we knew something.

They believed we were somebody else – doing something else. It was a case of mistaken identity. That was the only explanation. Nobody was going to assassinate the amok runners for just being ourselves. But I decided there and then to let them go on thinking whatever they wanted. I was going to get to the bottom of this little mystery – even if it killed me.

On the Wednesday, filming came to a sudden halt. A forest fire was blazing out of control across the Mae Ai hills and even though the flames were heading away from the ancient city set nobody could see a spear in front of their face through the smoke. The producers had hired a dozen truck tankers to ferry water from the Kok and hose down the area around the sets, just in case. OB had filmed one or two impromptu scenes that looked mysterious, like an old London fog, but having extras on the set didn't make a lot of sense if you couldn't see them. At eleven o'clock, the director called it a day.

We decided to drive back into Chiang Mai to see how Mair and granddad were doing and grab some clothes. Sissy was reversing out of the cobblestone driveway of our house when he suddenly slammed his foot on the brake.

'Nice driving,' said Arny.

But Sissy raised his chin at the rear-view mirror and we looked over our shoulders to see Bunny Savage dressed like Lara Croft. She was standing with her hands on her hips, her lovely legs akimbo in the open gateway. Arny smiled and nudged me.

'*Notting Hill*, buddy,' I said. 'Remember *Notting Hill*. She can't get you out of her mind.'

Sissy killed the engine and we climbed down.

'Princess,' said Sissy. He dropped to the ground and prostrated himself in front of her as he'd been taught by John Quirk. Arny did a shy finger wave from a distance. I walked up to her and shook her hand. It was soft and clammy.

'Don't touch my princess,' called Sissy from the gravel. He brandished his air saber and came at me. I produced my air submachine gun and shot him. He fell back against the jeep bleeding imaginatively.

'Yoo hoo. Anyone notice I'm standing here?' said the movie star.

'If you haven't got a weapon you can't play,' I told her.

'I've got bazookas,' she said and blushed at her joke.

'Yes you have but I don't think they count,' I said.

She smiled and put her hands in the pockets of her shorts.

'Well, I came to see if you guys were okay. I just got back. OB told me about your little explosion. I was worried.'

'Where you been, princess?' Sissy asked.

'Up on the Mekhong River floating candles,' she said. 'I'm serious. How are you both?'

'We're just a little singed,' I admitted.

'How's Khin?'

'She's good. We sent her back to Chiang Mai yesterday.'

'I like her.'

I took a step back and admired her costume.

'So, you're off to wrestle anacondas in the Amazon?' I asked.

'Like it?' She did a twirl.

'It's ... what's the word, Sissy?'

'Hot.'

'Yeah, that's it. If I were your mother I'm not sure I'd let you go out in public like it.'

She turned to Arny who was once more traumatized into silence.

'How's your back?'

'I'm taking painkillers,' he said.'

'Get yourself a decent lawyer and sue me,' said Bunny. 'I'm good for it.'

'Oh, I couldn't do that,' said Arny.'

'Where are you all off to?' she asked.

'We were just going down to Chiang Mai to visit the family,' said Arny.

'In that?' she asked.

'Jimm, she called my jeep a "that",' said Sissy.

'No offence,' said Bunny. 'I was just wondering how long it might take you. What's it got ... a ten CC engine?'

'What's your point, princess?' said Sissy.

'I could get you there an hour faster.'

The Lexus LX soared over the mountain roads ignoring fallen rocks, chickens and street signs. It was like watching the journey from a VIP cinema seat. We'd covered the flatland from Fang in the blink of an indicator button and were flying over the Chiang Dao hills on a two-lane road whose other vehicles seemed to be museum exhibits. White Terns surfed the Lexus slipstream. It was all perfect but for Gus.

Gus, the minder, had a back that never ended. His bald head grew from it like a mound of play dough. There didn't appear to be any moving parts up there.

His unblinking, unlashed eyes studied the road as he drove and on the rare occasion he spoke, the words were broadcast rather than enunciated. He appeared to be devoid of body hair but he was built like an armchair on oil drums so its absence didn't make him any less threatening.

I'd lost the jostle for the back seat so I sat beside him and tried to make conversation. But it was obvious the minder didn't see any hope for the world in people such as us. Sissy, in the meantime was giving Bunny the unexpurgated version of our family history, leaving out only Sissy. That seemed odd to me given how my brother loved to talk about himself. In fact I couldn't recall him being so jumpy in front of a woman. Celebrity was a threatening thing. It cloaked a person in a media-made aura that forced mere mortals to be somebody else. You were either obliged to act frighteningly cool and interesting, or defer and shower them with platitudes. Either way you looked like a dick.

There were two official stops in Chiang Mai for the Hollywood actress. We decided to tag along. The first was to the Ban Ging Gaew orphanage. We weren't surprised to see it wasn't a clandestine visit. Despite the short notice the world press was there to meet her. A gingery publicist rushed over to the car with a parasol. She shielded the star to an open-air but roofed area where everyone was gathered. Gus was always a pace behind her. We skulked from the car and stood unnoticed in the sunshine.

'I feel like ... used, man,' Sissy said.

'You mean she just wanted you and Arny there beside her in the car to make her look good?'

'It's the image thing,' said Sissy. 'Big car. A smooth guy on each arm.'

'I get it.'

'So, what do we do about … the information?' asked Arny, his eyes trained on his movie star.

One of the main objectives of this brief Chiang Mai visit was to chart the progress of the investigation of Boon's murder. We wouldn't go directly to the police. Rather, we'd get an update from my buddy on the crime desk at the *News*. Except I was supposed to be in Fang covering the movie so I couldn't go.

'Sissy, you should still see Nit like we planned,' I said.

'What? And leave Arny here alone with my girlfriend?'

'You don't think Guszilla's going to leave us alone for a second, do you?' said Arny. 'I doubt you have anything to fear.'

We walked under a shade tree in the orphanage grounds and watched the show. The babies at Ban Ging Gaew were neatly dressed, mostly in yellow, and sitting on the laps of the caregivers around a small cement quadrangle. The press was restricted to a central, taped off area. They could follow Bunny Savage with their cameras as she walked from baby to baby, cuddling, smooching, squeezing cheeks. It was theatre in the round except the audience was at the hub and the star orbited like a chess grandmaster.

'Look at her, Jimm,' said Arny.

'I am.'

'Doesn't that worry you?'

'No.'

'It worries me. Look at all that insincerity. You never know what you're really getting with an actress.'

'You worry too much,' I told him but I got the feeling that was the moment he decided not to have a relationship with Bunny Savage. I wondered how he was going to break it to her.

The next stop was to Umong Temple. We drove slowly so all the same press people could get there before us. There were much more splendid temples around Chiang Mai with more historical significance but the publicist had decided this one presented more photo opportunities. Bunny Savage in a moody temple cave; the candlelight glinting on a Buddha image. Bunny Savage on a wooden bridge feeding the consecrated turtles. Bunny Savage kneeling before the abbot, head bowed, hands together; the red and purple of her temporary sarong contrasting dramatically with the saffron. Wonderful colour magazine fodder. It had all been worked out.

'It's bullshit,' said Arny. We were sitting cross-legged under a *bo* tree watching the circus.

'You really think she's got any choice, brother?' I asked.

'Yes, she's got a choice. If she told the people round her to pack it in – stopped paying them or something – she could avoid all this crap. If she didn't enjoy it why would she do it?'

I hadn't seen Arny this animated since he came in second at the regional Body Beautiful competition the year before. The break up was already hitting him hard.

'You sound like you're taking this woman a wee bit too seriously, Arny,' said Sissy.

'Not at all. I just ... Oh, oh.'

A greasy-haired westerner in K-mart clothing decorated with heavy camera equipment broke away from the herd.

'You think he's coming for us?' Sissy asked.

'Looks like it,' I said. 'He's been eying us since we got out of the car. Could be the "Bunny Savage Secret Lover" shot.'

Sissy took Arny's hand and lifted it to his lips. He looked into his eyes and kissed his fingers. Arny giggled. Greasy stopped in his tracks, shook his head, and turned back to the circus.

Chapter 15

"Love means never having to say you're sorry."
Love Story (1970)

The show was over but two cars still tailed the Lexus. Gus hurried it along the narrow lanes but we were in town so there wasn't much chance to outrun anyone. We threaded along the back streets that led to the university. Gus seemed to be one of those new generation hard men brought up on computer games and arcades. He negotiated the natural obstacles like Luke Skywalker. By the time we hit Suthep Road and the back fence of CMU there was just the one car on our back. We stopped briefly to let out Sissy and he blew a kiss to Arny. Nobody bothered to follow him.

We turned left on the busy road. It was crammed with student motorcycles and the beaten up old cars of lecturers whom time and wealth had cruelly passed by. We swung into the back entrance to the university. We were supposed to sport a sticker allowing us access to the campus but Gus wound down the window and glared at the boy at the checkpoint. He was lost inside his uniform, overwhelmed by his responsibilities. Too much trouble – too little salary. He waved the big SUV through and saluted the frightening *farang* in the front seat. I'd assumed this would shake off our tail but the guard had lost all faith in his own authority and waved the Honda through also.

I had another idea. We drove across the campus where the beautiful old trees and landscaped grounds were slowly being gobbled up by building works and re-emerged through the main gate on Huay Gaew. We turned left, passed the zoo and headed up the hill to Doi Suthep. This was home turf. The Lexus made the slope of the mountain seem level but somehow the pursuers remained in sight. We passed the entrance to Khin's lane beside the Naval Station and climbed another two kilometres before executing a drastic U-turn. For a man with no neck Gus was an impressive driver.

We passed the press vehicle at speed, flew back down the hill and turned on two wheels into the lane. It was a job well done. Even Gus found some room on his face for a smile. The pursuit vehicle could only expect us to be heading back into the city. Gus slowed down along the lane and pulled up behind the house. When I suggested we go in for a cool drink until the coast was clear, I assumed Gus would be joining us. But I hadn't fully grasped the concept of serfdom. Bunny said, 'Gus, wait in the car.' And he waited in the car. Just like that. It put the bodyguard into an entirely different category in my mind. I'd been thinking of the big man as a functioning human being, but he wasn't. He was a military experiment – the perfect soldier, put down at the order of a mere girl. 'Gus, vacuum the carpet.' 'Gus, roll me another joint.'

In front of the peculiar house, Bunny Savage stood staring at the view. It was fuzzy, the way long-sightedness might interpret a city, but it was impressive never-the-less.

'It's still a bit smoky,' I said as Arny and I slid open the glass doors.

'I'm sure it's delightful in the winter,' she said. 'I imagine you all sitting here with your buddies like lords and ladies of the manor.'

'Pretty much,' I said and smiled at the sight of Bunny Savage on Khin's front deck. Weird. Not for the first time in my life I wished I had my own camera. At the *News* if I wanted photos I'd have to take a cameraman. It was a regulation. I didn't have one handy.

I'd left the fridge connected so there was cold coconut water in there that quenched our thirsts and cleared our pipes. At one stage, with Bunny negotiating the outside toilet, Arny marched over to me.

'Jimm, I don't think I can do it.'

'Do what, Arny?'

'Tell her we can't be together.'

'You wh…?'

'You know me. I don't like hurting people.'

'Arny, I don't think …'

'Can you do it for me? Please.'

He was dead serious. I guess when all you've ever known is women fawning over you, you assume we're all like that. So I promised to break the news to Bunny Savage; the woman who could have any man on earth.

'All right,' I said.

She came back from the latrine with a smile on her face.

'It's like being at camp,' she said.

'Was there paper over there?' I asked.

'Reams of it.'

'Won't be long,' Arny called from the far end of the house.

'Where are you going?' I shouted.

'Just to the store,' he said.

The nearest store was at the bottom of the mountain and I doubted Gus would be inclined to give him a ride. I ushered Bunny to the wooden bench beneath an iron filings tree. It provided some respite from the mid-afternoon sun. We sat opposite each other smiling.

'I could hang out here forever with you guys,' she said.

'You're certainly a step up from the type of company we usually get here.'

I suppose I could have just ignored my brother's request and pretended I'd broken up with her on his behalf. Of course there wasn't a hope in any of the Buddhist hells that she'd be thinking about dating him. I imagined her with the more pensive, more intelligent, more animated types. Guys who'd made fortunes with their nonce. Not a young man who'd spent more hours in a gym looking at himself in a mirror than in a classroom.

But I'd promised and Arny had a sixth sense when it came to lying to him. I'd never get away with it. He'd know. So, delicately, I approached the subject.

'Bunny?'

'Yes?'

'My brother.'

'Uhhu?'

'He's got it into his head that you like him romantically.'

'He's right.'

'Now, I reali ...What?'

'I do like him romantically.'

I was disappointed.

'Really? Why?'

'Jimm, are you kidding? He's unique. He's very attractive. And he doesn't see me as a bimbo.'

'But you wouldn't … I mean, you could never date somebody like that?'

'Why not? I think we'd have a cool time together. He's my type.'

'You can have your choice.'

'Of star hunters? Sure. But guys who aren't affected by the glitter, they're hard to find. Jimm, he's your brother so it's natural you don't see his best side. You grew up vomiting on each other and poking sticks up each other's butts. But your brother's real special. I'd date him at the drop of a hat.'

I was astounded. She'd rather lost a dimension in my mind's eye. But that made my next job even more difficult. I'd been charged with breaking the news to this gorgeous woman that Arny wouldn't go out with her. It was a delicate situation but I could only charge into it like a bull.

'Bunny, I'm sorry, but …'

Her cell phone rang.

As she fished it from her bag she said, 'Even the name's kind of quirky. What woman would imagine a lover with the name of Sissy?'

'I …?'

'Excuse me.'

She pressed *receive* and fell into a loud phone shout with someone almost out of cellular range. I knew my mouth was still open because a fly flew into it and I swallowed it.

Chapter 16

"Don't you find it a little bit (of a) coincidence that the body fell *perfectly* within the chalk outline on the floor?"
The Pink Panther (2006)

The matt-black Lexus dropped us off at the gate to the ski chalet house. The drive back had been uneventful. We'd picked up Sissy in front of the university and headed out to the mountains. Bunny sat in front with Gus. We fooled around in the back seat. Neither I nor Sissy had been free to tell our news. We'd said goodbye to Bunny who waved at us through the closed window. Arny mouthed, 'I'm sorry,' as they drove away and she looked blank. We'd tried to say goodbye to Gus who leaned forward to hide his left hand from his passenger and proffered us a middle finger. It probably annoyed him more that we found the gesture hilarious. So what if he did earn forty times more than we did? He was a man slave – no dignity in that.

'I got stuff to tell you,' Sissy said.

'Me too,' I replied.

We fumbled to unlock the front door, forgot where the light switches were and stumbled into the living room. I found one dimmer on the post in front of me and all the lights came on at once. There was a body on the Persian carpet. Arny screamed.

'That wasn't there when we left, was it?' Sissy asked.

'Oh, shit,' I said. 'This is very bad.'

We walked to the body. We weren't coroners but dead was dead. The man was middle-aged, Asian, well dressed, had a pained look on his face, dark skinned but drained. There was a bloodstain on the carpet that formed the shape of a lotus leaf around his head.

'Boys!' I said.'

'Yeah?'

'I think this is the perfect time to make this somebody else's problem.'

'I agree,' said Sissy.

'Arny, lock the front door.'

He didn't respond. He wasn't one for dead bodies.

'Arny,' I tried again. 'The door.'

That got him moving. We rolled our visitor in the carpet and tied it with curtain cords. We carried the package out to the deck, leaned it onto the balcony while we caught our breaths then toppled it over. There was one loud bang at the front door before the whole thing left its hinges and thumped to the floor. A dozen police officers – one with a video camera – charged into the house. They had their guns drawn. They hurried through the living room and surrounded us on the balcony. We were leaning nonchalantly against the rail. The cameraman rushed toward us and drowned us in a white light as the camera rolled. I raised two fingers behind Arny's head.

I recognized the Fang desk sergeant amongst the invaders. He stepped forward, confused, glanced over the rail into the dark water, looked at the three smiling inhabitants, and obviously didn't know what to say.

'Sergeant,' I said, 'is there some problem?'

'I ... er ... we heard there was some disturbance here,' he said. 'The neighbours alerted us.'

'They must have good hearing,' I said. 'There's nobody for half a mile.'

'Right,' he said. 'Well, they were passing and heard something. We were concerned for your safety given the events of last Monday.'

'Well, that's very nice of you,' said Sissy. 'I'll sleep so much better in my bed tonight in the knowledge that you're out there watching over us.'

There were policemen running in and out of rooms like the Keystone Cops. Chat looked over the balcony again. 'Perhaps we should just take a look around to be sure there are no intruders.'

'No,' said Arny.

We were no less surprised than the policeman by our little brother's interruption.

'What?' said Chat.

'I said, no!' replied Arny. 'Unless you have a warrant, of course. You don't, do you?'

'Not ... no.'

'Right then. You know the way out.'

We looked at our little brother with admiration. Cops came from the upper floors shaking their heads.

'Well, in that case ... sorry to have disturbed you,' said the policeman. He even saluted before turning back into the living room.

'Oh, sergeant,' Sissy called. Chat looked back over his shoulder. 'If you'd be kind enough to replace the front door before you go we'd sleep even more soundly.'

It took the police twenty minutes with improvised tools to re-hang the door. We sat on the recliners with our feet up and our backs to the action. When the last officer left and slammed the door behind him we did a quick reconnoitre of the house to be sure there weren't any left-over police hiding in the closets or under the bed. When we were certain we were alone we hurried to the balcony and leaned over. The river below was in shadow as the deck blocked off the lights from the house. I threw the switch to turn on the floodlights opposite. The warm green glow reached across the river and outlined the Persian carpet wedged on the rocks below us. In March the river ran low. The only spot one could really launch a body with any conviction was four or five meters in.

We scrambled down the bank.

'Just as well, I guess,' Sissy said. 'The carpet would have given us away eventually.'

'Huh, you think the local police could match a carpet to a house?' I said. 'They can hardly fill out a parking ticket.'

We unrolled our victim, pulled him out to the middle of the river, and sent him off downstream. He floated nicely. The hole in his head obviously hadn't let any of the air out of him. The current ran slowly but it had power. It carried off our unwelcome visitor, steered him around the bend and out of sight. We re-rolled the carpet around three large rocks and dragged it to the deepest point of the river. It sank as one would expect a four-thousand buck Persian wool carpet to sink. Even if some ranking police officer with an inkling were to return to the scene all he'd find would be a newly washed carpet and no body.

We waded back to the bank and sat breathing heavily as much from relief as from effort.

'There's a bright side to this,' I said.

'Oh, good,' said Arny.

'It tells us they don't think they can kill us anymore,' I said. 'If they did they'd just shoot us and throw us over the balcony. They wouldn't have gone to all this trouble to set us up. I think we're physically safe for the time being.'

'I don't feel particularly safe,' said Sissi.

'You did great, Arny,' I said. Sissy mussed his hair.

'You think maybe it's time for us to go home yet?' he asked.

'No, but I tell you what we need to do,' I said.

'What's that?'

'Take in tenants. The better-known the better. We don't want the gendarmes trying this one on us again.'

We climbed up to the balcony and sat on the recliners waiting for the shakes to go away. We were quiet for a while. Night creatures screeched and groaned and gurgled all around us. The river bubbled against the rocks. A truck with a faulty camshaft thumped over the distant bridge.

'Doesn't it get to you two?' Arny asked.

'What?' we asked.

'What we just did.'

'Throwing a dead body off the balcony?' said Sissy.

'Yeah.'

'It's starting to,' he said.

'I've got a serious wobble in my belly,' I told them. 'I need a shit and a shower, urgently.'

We all felt better after a soak and a glass of neat scotch. It wasn't a trauma that could be puffed away on a joint. "Scotch made a man of you, even if you started off as a woman." That was one of our granddad's favourite sayings. If you got the right whisky, a little matter of manhandling a corpse into a river could be seen as just a couple o' boys letting off steam. And we had the right whisky. The Swiss accountant was a good example of not being able to take it with you. He'd left a cabinet of expensive liquor. All the bottles had been opened but the contents barely touched, so he must have had a vision of his wife trying to sell them back to the liquor store. The cabinet had been securely fastened but my days on the crime desk had somehow turned me into a pretty good picklock. Arny threw back two wine coolers in record time. He wasn't the hard alcohol type. After a few sips of 18-year-old Talisker, Sissy and I were clear-headed enough to remember the two important matters of the day.

'What about Nit?' I asked.

'Yeah, right,' said Sissy. 'Forgot about Nit. He said hello and told me to remind you he's paying for a public interest assignment and not a murder enquiry. He tells me that over the past twenty-four hours the Chiang Mai cops haven't put out any new statements about Boon's killing. But he says there's a lot of pressure from Bangkok to find who offed him. The way they say it happened was like this: Boon was supposed to meet someone at Doi Chang coffee shop. The waitress girls said he was sitting there for a half hour looking at his watch and staring out the window. They recognized him from TV. Then he gets a call on his cell, pays and runs off out.'

'It was too public,' I said.

'Right. The investigators guess the killers called him back to the parking and terminated him there.'

'That doesn't make sense,' I said. 'You don't have to make an appointment with a guy to shoot him. Boon didn't have any security – no bodyguards. They could have killed him any time. I bet you something was supposed to be handed over there; papers, money or something, and it didn't happen.'

'Or it happened and they didn't need him anymore,' said Arny already slurring.

'Right,' I agreed. 'And it's all got to be connected with him staying in Fang after Siam wraps up. You know? I think we need to get a few more details about who he was dealing with up here. What kind of contract he had. I think we need to talk to his company again.'

'I'll call,' said Sissy.

'No,' I said. 'I don't get the feeling his secretary would tell us anything over the telephone. I need to go to Bangkok and talk to her personally – use my charm.'

'You haven't got charm, sister,' said Sissy. 'This is a job for Casanova here. I'll go. You hold the fort here.'

With Arny there on the balcony with us I couldn't tell Sissy about our weird afternoon. Or perhaps I just didn't think it was that urgent. But I wondered how innocent my gender bender brother had been in the whole affair. If I didn't know better I'd say he'd been flirting.

'Have you noticed how heavily you've been leaning on your alter ego of late?' I asked.

'What do you mean?'

'Just that I'm wondering whether that chest tape might have made you forget you have breasts.'

'Don't be ridiculous. I'll go as a woman. I'm even more charming as a girl.'

'If you're sure.'

'Next break in filming,' he said.

'That could be two weeks off,' said Arny.

'Did you see the stupa on top of Tha Ton hill when we drove in?' I asked.

'Can't say I noticed,' said Sissy.

'You wouldn't have seen it,' I said. 'The mountain's just a blur and if it doesn't rain overnight I've got a feeling tomorrow's going to be another rest day. No-one's in a rush to put the fires out.'

'Okay. Then tomorrow it is. I'll take the Suzuki.'

'Did you get a chance to talk to Nit about the CCTV idea?' I asked.

'Yeah,' said Sissy. 'He was into it. His neighbor's wife's a cleaner at the Dhara Dhevi. She knows the security guy. They've only got two cameras: one in reception and one in the parking lot. They keep the tapes for a month so he should have the two guys that walked through reception that night, then one more when they get in their car. The News has agreed to pay for copying the film. They'll make stills of the two guys and run them in the paper for as long as they can till the cops come and shut 'em down. They hope they'll get an ID before then. He'll send us copies when he gets ...'

There came an almighty crash from the front of the house. Fearing the worst, we all leapt from our recliners and looked nonchalant. But even in a state of panic none of us spilled our eighteen-year-old scotch. We strolled back into the house and found the front door lying on the ground, and a lanky confused Burmese in a brand new pink skirt. Khin stood in the empty door frame with one fist in front of her.

'Khin, you mountain woman,' said Sissy. 'Don't you know your own strength?'

'I merely knocked,' Khin replied. 'Even where I come from these things have hinges.' She walked on top of the door and between us. 'I can't tell you how problematic it's been finding you. I don't suppose you have a kitchenette here? I could eat a horse – a large one.'

What the larder lacked in horses it made up for in instant noodles. Khin had two bowls steaming in front of her. We three sat on the far side of the chic Fleig table waiting for the next utterly predictable instalment of her story. We'd heard so many chapters it was starting to sound like one of the fifties radio dramas that spun out their far-fetched yarns for a decade before fizzling out with the sponsorship fees. The Burmese spoke between slurps.

'Yes,' she began. 'I have in fact spent the previous two nights working by candlelight in the musty underground manuscript room at Suan Dork Temple. I have befriended no end of entomological specimens. But deep in the shelves I found two manuscripts that were devoted to the biography of your beloved monarch, Mangrai.'

'Go grandpa,' said Sissy.

'They were dated 1629 but they would naturally have been rewritten from earlier versions. They were resplendent with details of the despot's jolly adventures around the region. Were you aware, for example, that he acquired some three-hundred concubines in his travels?'

'Wow,' said Sissy. 'The guy must have died before he hit thirty.'

'In actual fact, (Khin avoided humour whenever possible), he lived to the ripe old age of seventy-nine.

He passed away on a shopping expedition at Chiang Mai's central market in 1317.'

Sissy laughed.

'Can't you just see him, Jimm? Wandering through the market with his three hundred wives? Honey, get me a dress. Honey, look at those shoes. Aren't they just me?'

A slightly pickled Arny joined in.

'Can you believe that?' he said. 'He survives endless battles against the Mongols and dies shopping. There's a message there for us single guys.'

Khin used this frivolous hiatus to slurp up several forkfuls of slithery noodles and wash them down with whisky.

'I found a great deal of fascinating data,' she continued, a worm of pasta dangling from the corner of her mouth. 'But there were only two mentions of the Sikanchai dagger. Don't forget, the dagger is the key. Find the dagger and we have the treasure.'

I yawned behind my hand.

'One entry referred to its use at the coronation during the establishment of Chiang Mai. Of this we have already learned, except that there was a direct reference to all the coronation regalia being protected by the men of the Royal Plaza. These were the ceremonial guards, the Thai equivalent of England's Beefeaters, and they were certain to have been based in the ancient city whilst King Mangrai was active there.'

She scooped up more noodles, let them settle in her big mouth then reached for her Abibas day pack on the floor at her feet. She pulled out a Hello Kitty lined notebook and flipped through the pages.

'Yes,' she said. 'So we come to the second mention. You have to remember that the texts were written in ancient Shan.'

'Which you happened to have picked up on the flight from Yangon,' Sissy threw in.

'It's quite a straight-forward language. Grammatically logical but rather flowery. It's similar to Thai in many ways. It's very much open to interpretation but it seems to say something like this: "In the regent's declining years," Khin read, "he spent more time in the water city, and there it was he put the kin of the dagger to rest". That's my starting off point.'

'So it didn't exactly say "the Sikanchai dagger" then?' I pointed out.

'It is implied.'

'Khin,' I said, 'don't you think you're trying just a little too hard to make the facts fit the dreams?'

'I assure you this is the dagger we're seeking.'

I looked her in the eye. 'Sister, you're a researcher. You have to see what's actually there in front of you, not what you hope's there.'

'It is there, Jimm.'

'Okay, so it's there,' Arny was impatient. 'Where's the water city?'

'Ah, good question,' she said. 'There is no other mention of the water city in any of the other texts, but here's my calculated guess. Before founding Chiang Mai, King Mangrai built a walled city to its south at a bend in the Ping river. He lived there on and off, even after the establishment of Chiang Mai as the capital of his kingdom. If the location had been less problematic it would have been the capital of Lanna and not Chiang Mai.'

'Wiang Kum Kam,' I said.

Arny raised his eyebrows. 'How'd you know that?'

'I've been there,' I said, 'on a story. It's a dozen piles of bricks off the road to Lamphun. I'd been expecting Angkor Wat but all I got was a building site.'

Khin shook her head. 'To really *see* Wieng Kum Kam you have to wear your uncynical X-ray glasses. You have to realize that some of these bricks were laid seven-hundred years earlier. The buildings were erected by slaves and soldiers in the days before back hoes and cranes. If you look at Wieng Kum Kam and see a building site then you have been deprived one of the most profound experiences of living in Chiang Mai. When they first discovered the ruins in 1978 it was all I could do not to sneak across the border and come to see them myself. I could hardly contain my excitement.'

She was still unable to contain her excitement. She waved her long fingers in front of her like the blades of Edward Scissorhands. Her voice rose to a pitch. Her noodles sat neglected. We watched her enthuse and I wondered when my own passion had died. I wondered when I'd last experienced a thrill at the thought of performing a task. When did all my bubbles go flat? I needed Khin around with her lust for knowledge and her far-fetched theories just to stop myself from dropping into a deep sleep and never waking up.

'I'll try harder next time,' I said. 'Sorry, Khin.'

Sissy had no patience with diversions. 'So, Mangrai built this city under water?'

'No, Sissy.' Khin often addressed my brother as would a high school teacher speaking slowly for the benefit of the dumb kid in the back row. 'When they built the city it was on dry ground. But every monsoon season the river rose higher until it reached the stage where the city was flooded for two or three months a year. Thailand has a history of establishing cities in totally inappropriate places. Bangkok itself is constantly investing in flood reparations. Chiang Mai's own downtown spends several weeks under water every ...'

'Khin, the water city!' Sissy snapped.

'Yes,' said Khin. 'So my interpretation of the manuscripts is that, in his dotage, Mangrai spent more and more time in his original city and left the running of Chiang Mai and Lanna to the nobles. Lamphun was once a very religious, almost sacred part of the country. It is said the Lord Buddha spent much time there himself. And it was this fact that drew Buddhist scholars from near and far. Many Mangrai dynasty leaders dedicated their twilight years to the faith. Wieng Kum Kam was a small area no more than a square kilometer in its heyday, but it contained and was surrounded by some forty temples. I can visualize Mangrai there away from the chaos of the city, making his peace with the Lord ...'

'Up to his knees in flood water,' Sissy added.

'Reading the scriptures, dictating his memoirs,' Khin continued. 'It would have been the ideal spot – the perfect setting for laying the souls of the Mangrai treasure to rest. I am certain that's where it will be found.'

'Based on reading about something that might have been the Sikanchai dagger in a place that might have been Wieng Kum Kam,' I said.

'Jimm, I have told you a number of times that history is not a science,' she said. 'It's an interpretation of collaborating evidence. The war in Vietnam as written by the CIA and the Viet Khong, are two vastly different wars. A good historian is one who can sift through the propaganda and balderdash and be left with what can only be true. It's an analysis of all the material available. I can look at an event that took place yesterday and observe that news reports vary from around the world depending on a country's bias and political stance. The further back we travel in time, the more we are left with accounts of events that were written by scribes commissioned by the rulers of the time. Of course, every king will be bold and valiant if he's writing his own history.

'Then there were the monks,' she continued. 'They wrote their versions of events based on rumours and tittle-tattle from travelling merchants. Is it possible that everything written in and about the thirteenth century was a lie? Of course it is. There are those who believe everything they read. There are others who read two or three versions and draw a compromise. And there are historians who look at everything, analyze it, and refer to scientific and geographical data to eliminate the impossible. As Sherlock Holmes said, once the improbable has been eliminated, what you are left with, however illogical, has to be the truth. I am left with a dagger and a water city and I ask myself, why would the scribe bother to mention these two if they are irrelevant, and why would they survive numerous rewritings?'

After one more pause to be certain Khin had finished her lecture, we got to our feet and applauded. Khin harpooned a last knot of cold noodles and scooped them into her mouth without a nod of recognition.

'Khin, you're a one-off,' I said. 'Only you could support a closing argument with a quote from a fictional character created by a guy famous for hoaxing the scientific community.'

'I have a knack.'

'You sure do.'

'Now, where am I sleeping?' she asked.

'Wait, what are you doing here?' Sissy asked.

'I am in transit,' she said.' I shall be relocating anon to Wieng Kum Kam. I wanted to update you on my progress and assure myself that you could survive here without my protection. One can only hunt treasure when one has peace of mind.'

Chapter 17

"This city is afraid of me. I have seen its true face."
Watchmen (2009)

It was early. We'd become used to the 5AM bells that shook the monks from their heavenly slumber and sent them off on their rounds. We were immune to the hoarse braying of the cocks and the pops of the early bamboo bonfires. But it wasn't long after these that I entered into an erotic dream about the raspy tongue of a rugged Burmese infantryman licking my thigh. I'd never been that fond of foot soldiers till then. I was awoken by a warm damp feeling in my lap where a rogue cat had chosen to end her night wanderings. I didn't have the energy to swipe her off. It was then that Arny came banging on my door to tell me the shoot was off and we were free for another day.

Wieng Kum Kam was a difficult concept for a foreign visitor to take in. One would have to imagine a place like the ancient monoliths of Stonehenge in the south of England with no rules. Rather than the vast expanse of land surrounding the site, you have a housing estate. The backyards of the houses abut the stones. Perhaps one household extends from one side of an arch to the other and visitors have to ask permission from the householder to go through their back gate and take a look.

Such was the value of real estate close to Chiang Mai that the ruins coexisted with a clutter of private residences. Many treated the brick piles like garden ornaments. Children played soccer amid the foundations and stood up ancient steps as goal posts. Dogs sprawled on temple pediments giving no mind at all to the fact they'd been crafted seven hundred years earlier. A motorcycle leaned against a half-constructed stupa. Washing hung across the entrance to a temple. There was nothing grand about the place at all – narrow streets, small houses, compact sites. But still the tourist trade flourished in its way. Ponies and traps once popular in Lamphun and Lampang had relocated to Wieng Kum Kam. There was a standard tour from one abandoned dig to the next. The drivers had no English so the visitors were obliged to buy a photocopied map at the restaurant and attempt to match it to the sites. It was no easy task as the temples and chedi's on the map were spectacular and complete whereas the remains were neither. There were stops for ice cream on the way and souvenirs. Who knew? Perhaps one of the pebbles for sale in the zip lock plastic bag was an actual relic from a kingdom of old Wieng Kum Kam.

To my eyes it was just depressing. We all sat in the hot Suzuki at the official starting point of the tour: me, Khin and Arny. We'd dropped off Sissy at Chiang Mai airport and he'd managed to get a late standby ticket on Nok Air to Bangkok. He'd handed the car keys to me and told me to keep the radiator topped up. Suzukis had a habit of overheating. I drove the twenty kilometres south to Wieng Kum Kam with my foot on the accelerator and my eye on the oil and temperature gauges.

The complex was laid out in front of us, a rubble field to me, an historical orgasm to Khin. As far as I was concerned the only element of wonder about the site was the remote possibility that under one of these suburban rockeries there might be a billion dollars worth of treasure. But with Khin as my guide I knew it was an ill-conceived fancy. There was no more chance of digging up sacks of gold in this graveyard of history than there was of finding King Mangrai alive in the rubble. Khin seemed capable of ignoring the march of the suburbs and notice only the debris of glories past. She was insistent on leading her guests on a walking tour.

Arny was both fascinated by Khin's inexhaustible knowledge of Lanna history and stimulated by some unseen energy from the sites. To my frustration he seemed to see it all. Everything Khin described was real to him. There were no dressmaker's stalls or noodle sellers. No internet cafes around him. Like Khin, he was able to visualize with his heart just as she had promised. I walked through the ancient city like an actor in a blue screen studio not knowing what wonders might be superimposed there. I tagged along behind, muttering curses under my breath. We sat on a concrete slab in front of Ma Gluer Temple. Arny looked up to where he visualized the tiered roof reflected gold against the sixteenth century sky. But at the end of a very long guided tour of bricks, I was ready to bury the Burmese and forget about the possibility of riches beyond my imagination.

'Okay, ma'am,' I said to Khin. 'How can we get rid of you now?'

'I think a visit to the palm leaf manuscripts in Lamphun would be in order,' she said. 'I need further clues to help me ascertain which of the Wieng Kum Kam temples held some special affection in the heart of

King Mangrai. If he had a favourite, I am certain he would have erected a tope in its grounds. And that, my friends, is where he would have buried his treasure.'

Arny squeezed my arm. 'Isn't it thrilling?'

'A buzz a minute, I said. 'Tell me, Khin. Why the hell don't you just hire yourself a metal detector and run it over all the sites here?'

Khin shook her head as if she'd given up hope of ever finding another human with common sense.

'Don't you suppose some half a million souvenir hunters might have already been here since this dig was unearthed?' she said. 'And let us analyze their effectiveness. Firstly, the detectors they use to hunt for coins on the beach in this country are probably effective to a depth of no more than eight inches. A national treasure would have been buried deep below the base of a stupa – perhaps six feet or more. Secondly, any valuables would have been caked in some type of solid material.'

'They buried it in cement?' I asked.

'Some form of plaster, more like. Cement wasn't invented until …'

'I was kidding, Khin.'

'Yes. Very amusing.'

'Thanks. So when do you want to start the search?'

'I always adhere to the maxim that there is no time like the present,' she said. 'I have my advance from the sadly deceased film director and my compensation from the Americans so there is nothing holding me back.'

'Then I'll take you down to Lamphun town and dump you there,' I said.

'Too kind.'

Chapter 18

"Bad luck, I guess. It floats around. It's got to land on somebody."
The Shawshank Redemption (1994)

There was the smell of incense in Khin's old Doi Suthep house early the next morning. It floated across from the grounds of Sri Soda Temple. That was a busy old temple at around 6AM. A whole legion of monks and novices shuffled their way down past the zoo on their alms route. It was the Buddhist equivalent of drive-in banking. Busy Chiang Mai'ans drove their cars to the fitness park and waited beside the road for a chain of saffron that didn't exceed the number of food portions they had in the trunk of the car. They'd hop out, fill the alms bowls, get blessed and be back home in time to catch the seven-o'clock news bulletin. For those who didn't have the time to prepare any food, there were roadside monk takeaways available for a small fee. You could even hire someone to donate the alms for you and stay in bed. Buddhism was nothing if not accommodating.

'Good news,' said Arny, again waking me from a deep sleep. 'The smoke's cleared enough to shoot. They're starting at noon. They need both of us.'

'Too bad' I said. 'Hey! Do they pay for days off?'

'Sure they do.'

'So can't we stay in bed?'

It was the clearest day yet at the shoot sight. The locals told them it hadn't exactly been a gale that blew the smoke away, more a kind of draft. It wasn't even strong enough to get tinkles out of a wind chime. But it had sufficient oomph to lean on the smoke and move it along. OB decided to film one of the major scenes while they could still see each other. It was the great confrontation from the point of view of the good guys. The extras were decked out in yellow, not because it had much bearing on allegiances in the 16th century but because it looked good on screen. When they turned Burmese in a few days, the extras would be in red.

One of two problems OB encountered that day was getting all the extras to run in the same direction at the same time. For some reason they found it difficult to retreat or attack as one. They advanced at a walk with no problem but when it came to running, some just turned tail and fled. Perhaps it was in their DNA. It was something OB hoped would be sorted out over time.

The other problem they had that day was Dan Jensen deciding he wanted Tony, his pet shi tzu, to have a role in the film. And to complicate matters, as if that wasn't complicated enough, he wanted him in the battle scene. OB pointed out that sixteenth century generals rarely went off to war with their lap dogs at their side. Jensen got into a sulk, threatened to walk and left OB no choice but to conjure up another impromptu scene - Tony snatched from the path of a raging bull elephant at the last second. It was dramatic and emotional and would be on the cutting room floor as soon as OB could find the scissors. It all wasted another hour but still they might have got the day's shoot in the bank before sundown if only they hadn't experienced problems with two of the main cameras.

The technicians couldn't work out the glitch. They'd start filming a scene and the things would freeze up; both of them, simultaneously. It was as if something about the temperature or the humidity was clogging up the works. Someone suggested it could be the dust in the atmosphere, but these were six-hundred-thousand dollar cameras. They'd filmed in sandstorms in the middle of the desert. Nobody could understand how a little air dust could shut them down.

OB had worked on projects like this before – hexed movies. The line director and producers would follow him around the set reminding him how far over budget they were going.

'Don't tell me. Tell God,' he'd say.

Once the gremlins were out of their box he knew the timetable was doomed and there wasn't a thing he could do about it. There were directors who'd hit the cast and crew over the head with crow bars if things stopped running smoothly. But this was OB. He'd been around the block twice and been mugged a few times on the way. He was past caring now. He didn't hear the whining. He had enough money and enough success. He had nothing to prove. He just loved making magic with a camera. He'd do it for nothing. And once the day was over and he'd gone through the rushes he didn't want to go to meetings with money guys and defend himself. Money guys could always find more money and there'd never be enough profits.

All he wanted at the end of a work day was to sit, have a little drink or a little smoke and talk shit. Perhaps that was why he was so easily sold on my idea. The cameras had jammed. They'd ordered replacements from Bangkok. We were all sitting around hoping that repeatedly prodding the same button might bring the machines back to life. OB had seen me sitting on an earthen rampart reading. He'd come over to join me. I was flattered he remembered me.

'How you doing, Jimm?' he asked.

'Pretty good.'

'How's the book?'

'Gory. The history of Fang. Thai Tourism Authority writers have a way of glamorizing drugs and death.'

'You do any writing yourself?'

'Nah,' I said. I hadn't told him I was there as a reporter. Thought it would be better kept to myself.

'I made the mistake of learning to read before I learned to write. Since then I've had no choice but to compare myself to others. I've never worked out how good writers make it all look so easy. I'm a reader and proud of it.'

'I hear you've found a new place to stay,' he said.

'Yeah. It's heaven. On the river. No neighbours. All modern conveniences. Six bedrooms with on-suites. AC in all of them. Scant Swiss furnishings. Stocked booze cabinet.'

'You sound like you're selling it.'

'I'm looking for housemates. Know anyone? There's just me and my brothers in there. We could use some company. We need cheering up.'

'We're all a bit down after a day like this.'

'Yeah, I saw you rescue the ugly Chinese dog from the jaws of death. I think it'll make the movie. It could be to *Siam* what the shower scene was to Psycho. I don't know how you do it.'

'Rescue dogs?'

'Juggle all the egos. I mean, who is this guy? He gets known on some TV show and suddenly he thinks he's Richard Burton. He goes around with his frigging entourage holding everyone to ransom. Give me a break.'

OB laughed.

'The glamour only affects a small percentage of them, Jimm. And, you'll be pleased to know they're the ones that land with the biggest bump when it's all over.'

We sat smiling in silence for a while looking around at the expanse of extras in their cross-legged circles playing cards, eating, a game of rattan ball here, a soccer match there. They were happy – getting paid to do nothing. Who wouldn't be? Even the elephants ripping vegetation from the hillsides seemed content.

'Jimm?'

'Yeah?'

'You got an age limit for that tenant of yours?'

So, that was it. When Sissy arrived back at the house that evening there was already a Thai military type manning the closed gate. He had a gun in a holster and a clipboard.

'I live here,' Sissy told him.

'Can I have your name, sir?'

'No, I might need it again.'

There was no sign that the man had registered this as a joke. Sissy dropped his head and spelt out his surname which happened to be the same as mine. The guard unfastened the bolt and gave him just enough space through which to negotiate the Suzuki. He parked beside a Land Rover and a familiar Lexus. Gus looked up briefly from the driver's seat and then returned to his i-pod without acknowledging Sissy. A second security person sat on a plastic chair under the *lumyai* tree. Sissy was impressed. He threw his Abibas over his shoulder and walked to the front door. Even that was new – more tasteful than its predecessor and twice as thick. It was ajar.

The sound of piano jazz ran like a warm rinse through the house. He had no idea who it was. He preferred country ethnic in his own language. Jazz frustrated him. He wished the guys would just settle on a melody and stick to it. But he tolerated it because he'd been exposed to it for so long. He'd had a German husband for a while. He'd learned the language, the icons, the mannerisms, the music. Yet, like me, he could never get it completely right because he was Thai. We'd grown up switching codes. Mair had given us a bilingual upbringing that wasn't quite complete. We almost spoke English like natives – almost spoke Thai like Thais. But the culture police, they were sharp, man. They caught you out every time. We made mistakes all across the board and they spotted them. So we'd never really been one or the other with any conviction.

He walked to the balcony and there we all were. All six recliners had been dragged into a line parallel to the river and five of them were occupied. The floodlights had turned the far bank into a luminous green arboretum. From the rear the observers seemed frozen in fascination at its glow. I was one of the starers, then Bunny Savage, Arny, OB the director, and finally Kuro the Japanese-Thai King.

I looked around to find my brother staring at us.

'You've gone to extreme lengths to make the house police-proof,' he said in Thai.

'Aha,' said I. 'Sissy's here. We have a full house.'

The guests seemed to rise in slow motion to greet him. Bunny alone appeared particularly animated at his arrival but that was probably because she was drinking beer rather than imbibing in our very special weed.

'What kept you?' she said.

Sissy had that thick head that comes from driving on Thai roads at night. The news that you were supposed to dip your headlights hadn't made it to the people who passed their driving tests with a cheque book.

'I don't get out of second gear after dark,' Sissy said. 'Evening, folks.'

We all *wai*'d him in our respective ethnic fashion. It was a mishmash of odd salutes but he was obliged to *wai* us back. He did it Chinese style like in the kung fu movies. Kuro was the only one of the group he hadn't met before. He shook the actor's hand and used some of the Japanese lines he'd picked up from his Tokyo salary men boyfriends in the good old days.

'Solly, I do not speak Thai,' Kuro said.

If he hadn't actually been Japanese, his accent wouldn't have fooled anyone. Sissy was stymied for a moment until the actor laughed.

'Just kidding,' he confessed. '*Kon ban wa.*'

'I'm stuck with comedians everywhere I go,' Sissy shook his head. 'I'm gonna get myself a beer. I'll be back.'

He walked to the kitchen and said hello to two Thai women in uniform sitting at the dining table. They stood when he came in.

'Who are you?' he asked.

'We work here,' they said, almost in sync. 'What can we get you, sir?'

Sissy thought that was very funny.

'Nothing, girls,' he laughed. He walked to the fridge and opened the door. It looked like a display cabinet at Harrods.

'Damn.'

'We've moved up a peg, pal,' I said.

I'd followed him into the kitchen. The serving wenches fled.

'You're something else, Jimm,' he said.

'Anything from Bangkok?' I asked.

'Plenty.'

Sissy selected a Belgian Stella Artois and even put it in a glass. We sat at the table.

'Okay, let's have it.'

'What about the guests?' he asked.

'They aren't guests, Sissy. They live here.'

'All of them? How'd you swing that?'

'Have you seen the rooms at the Chalet?'

'I've seen the rooms at the Dhara Dhevi.'

'None of them wants to share a chopper with Jensen back into town,' I said. They'd sooner stay here. It's a home. We're a family. OB and Kuro have the two master bedrooms on this floor and you and me and Arny keep our penthouse suites upstairs.'

'We're missing a queen,' he said.

'Ah, find the lady. Now that's something I have to talk to you about.'

'Okay,' Sissy said. 'But I'll tell you about Bangkok first while I can still remember it all. I've got a highway headache so bear with me.'

'Go for it.'

'Boon's movie,' he said, 'the one they were going to make after Siam, it was from a classic Thai historical story. They showed me the script.'

'You didn't have to sleep with the personal secretary to get it, I hope.'

'She was two-foot-six with a ring through her lip and a poster of that French lady tennis player above her desk. So, no, I got all this by hard work and natural charm. We did some gay/lesbian bonding. She told me the movie was going to be a King Mangrai against the Mongols epic. A buddy movie.'

'The three kings?'

'You've got it. All the politics and rivalry and eventual friendship of these three rival royals who band together and beat back the Chinese hoards.'

'So, Boon let us give him a Lanna history lesson even though he knew it all?'

'I guess he just liked listening to our version of it. It was a good idea. Potentially good cinema. But it was a way too ambitious movie for the company. They didn't have the backing. They needed to cut costs.'

'So that's when they decided to negotiate with the Americans,' I said.

'Right. And that's when things started to go crazy.'

'They had to pay tea money to someone in country to get a deal?'

'Yeah', he nodded, 'but that was expected. You write that kind of thing into the budget out here. It was covered. They even had the funds to keep all the extras on for two more days after *Siam*. They couldn't pay them as much as Hollywood but that wasn't a problem. They were probably grateful for any extra money they could get during the dry season. It was a kind of bonus.

Those that didn't think it was worth it were free to turn round and go home. If they still had a thousand men for the battle scenes it would have worked.'

'So, what went wrong?' I asked.

'They don't know. Boon met with the Northern Thai Castings rep twice. The emails Boon sent back to Bangkok were all promising. NTC had agreed to the daily rate for extras and even reduced costs for transport and catering. Thais looking out for Thais. Everything was on track. Even up to the day we met Boon at the Dhara Dhevi it still looked rosy. But the day after that, they lost contact with him.'

'Did they know about the meeting at the coffee shop?'

'Not a thing.'

'Shit. Did she say whether the police went to see them?'

'After the murder?'

'Yeah.'

'No. Nobody from Chiang Mai contacted them at all.'

'So the official line is …?'

'Business deal gone bad.'

'And everyone accepts that?' I asked.

'It's a good old Thai cliché. Who's going to argue?'

'Did he have a wife … girlfriend? Anyone he could confide in?'

'Divorced. Lived in a room above the company office. His only romance was with his work. These people do twenty-three hours a day. Their only family's their crew.'

I thought about it for a while.

'That's it,' I said.

'What?'

'His crew. They were close. They drank together. I bet he told someone on his team what was going on.'

'It's possible,' he said. 'I'll go talk to them at the shoot tomorrow. That's if I haven't been fired for playing hooky for two days.'

'The big guy's our roommate now,' I reminded him.

'You're right. Let's go suck up.'

'First I need to tell you something disturbing about …'

We were interrupted by Arny who walked clumsily into the kitchen.

'You two leaving me alone to entertain those big wigs?' he asked with an odd smile on his face.

'Arny, are you stoned again?' Sissy asked.

'Little bit,' he said. 'It's for medicacinismal purposes for my back. The doctor recommended it.'

'Stick around, brother,' said Sissy. 'Jimm's got some big news for me.'

'Ah, that's okay,' I said. 'It'll keep.'

Even though at the time I was afraid it wouldn't.

Every now and then, we would lean forward and stare at the river to see whether any Persian motifs shimmered beneath the surface of the water under the glimmer of the lights. It was midnight. OB and Arny had retired. Bunny had gone upstairs also but she said she'd just be reading her script for the morning. We were left alone with Kuro and the hovering shadows of two housekeepers. The Japanese seemed impervious to smoke and booze which made us question whether he was really Japanese. He was our kind of man – laid back and funny. We tried to convince him to apply for a job at the Fuji restaurant at Airport Plaza so we could hang out after the movies. He told us he'd think about it.

'One of my derights,' he told us, 'is to rearn about different culture. I enjoy to gain knowledge about the world in such a way. It is my legret that I cannot communicate with the soldiers on the shoot.'

'The extras?' Sissy asked.

'Yes. They do not speak any ranguage we can discover. Not Thai. Not Burma. Somebody tell me they are Shan-Thai. They have transrator but transrator does not have time for social, is it … chit chat?'

It was the first we'd thought about it. We'd assumed the extras were tribesmen from minority communities. There were several ethnic groups clustered along the Thai border and we didn't speak any of their languages. But a gathering of two thousand guys and none of them speaking Thai? The odds against that were phenomenal. Sissy looked at me. We'd both tried to engage the extras in conversation and been met with blank expressions. We'd assumed they didn't want to talk to strangers or they'd been told not to. We hadn't considered the fact they might not have been able to. They were certainly worth another visit.

In order to contemplate the matter more thoroughly, Sissy announced he was off to pay homage to the ancestors at the porcelain shrine. Kuro waited until he was gone.

'Your brother is quite unusual,' he said.

'Some people might say weird,' I told him.

Chapter 19

"I love women. Wearing their clothes makes me feel closer to them. "
Ed Wood (1994)

It was a while before I realized Sissy had gone straight to bed. And by then it was too late to warn him. I doubted he'd ever forgive me. This is his version of what transpired that night.

He'd had a shower in his en-suite and put on his thick towelling robe against the air-conditioning. When he went back into his room he was surprised to see Bunny Savage sitting in the arm chair beside the bed. She had on a silk yukata and she wasn't being too modest about how she wore it. Sissy smiled.

'Hello,' he said.

'Hope you don't mind,' said Bunny.

'Not at all,' said Sissy, still blissfully unaware of his visitor's intentions. He sat on the bed and dried his hair; two girls about to share secrets at a slumber party.

'You're different,' said Bunny.

'Thank you,' said Sissy.

'You know I don't usually do this.'

'Do what?'

'Sneak into a strange man's room uninvited.'

'You don't need an invite, Little Sister. My door's always open. Jimm used to come in all the time for confessionals.'

'That's a little bit different, don't you think?'

She looked offended.

'Is it?' said Sissy.

'I heard that you were interested in me.'

'Are you kidding? I'm crazy about you. You've got everything I've ever wanted.'

Bunny got up from the armchair and sat very close to my brother on the bed.

'Really' she asked.

'Absolutely,' he said and squeezed her hand. 'You can tell me anything.'

'You know, I believe I can. That's what makes you different.'

She went to kiss him and he instinctively offered her his cheek. She was confused but persistent.

'Do you mind if I stay here tonight?'

'Not at all,' said Sissy.

'You're so … so natural.'

'Oh, there are one or two unnatural bits.'

She laughed.

'Can I use your bathroom to freshen up?' she said, and licked her top lip before leaving the bedroom. That was the moment Sissy had his revelation. The clumsy silk yukata had sailed through the radar without a blip. But the top lip lick? He'd used that same gesture on a number of occasions with remarkable success. It was something men responded to. He'd never use it with a girlfriend.

When the bathroom door closed he rewound the tapes of his memory and came to the scary conclusion that he'd screwed up monumentally. Bunny Savage was attracted to him as a man. It was unthinkable that a woman would recognize enough male characteristics in him to tickle her libido. But there it was. It was unlikely she'd consider a lesbian relationship and she was far too feminine for his taste, sexually. It was a difficult situation. He knew he had to be gentle if he wanted to avoid hurting her feelings. He didn't want to lose her as a girl friend and without a little tact the whole thing might blow into a thoroughly humiliating experience.

Bunny emerged from the bathroom with her robe unfastened. She was naked beneath. Her hair was swept back as if she'd been riding a motorcycle without a helmet. Sissy stood in the middle of the room holding his wallet out in front of him.

'What do you have there?' she asked.

'Some pictures I'd like you to see,' said Sissy. He'd considered stripping off and lying naked on the bed but thought that might be a tad too drastic for the situation. Bunny came and stood beside him, linking her arm through his.

'This is us as kids,' he said, showing the first photo.

'You were adorable even then,' she said. 'Look at you with your flowery hat.'

'Thank you. It was my favourite hat.' He flipped to the next picture. 'And this is our mother, Mair and my Grandad Jah.'

Her hand was stroking his arm.

'It's adorable that you carry family photos around with you,' she said.

'Yes,' said Sissy. He flipped to the last picture. It showed a glamorous girl in a low-cut gown. She had a sparkly tiara on her head and wore a sash with Thai characters on it.

'She's cute,' said Bunny. 'Old girlfriend?'

'Not exactly,' said Sissy.

'Wait,' said Bunny. 'Why have you chosen this exact moment to show me …? She's not your ex?'

'No.'

Bunny pulled away.

'So she's the reason you haven't wrestled me onto the bed?'

'You could say that.'

Bunny collected together the flaps of her yukata and tied the cord.

'You don't think you might have mentioned the fact you're in love with someone else before you let me make a fool of myself?'

She headed for the door.

'Well, Bunny,' said Sissy. 'That's just it. 'I hadn't suspected for a second that you were interested in me in that way. We all thought you had a thing for Arny.'

'Arny? Are you fucking kidding me?'

'He's a sweet boy.'

'He's meat.'

She turned the door handle.

'And what's with the "You've got everything I've ever wanted," routine?'

'That's absolutely true. I want your body. Your face. Your magnetism. Your voice. Your career. Your income. I want everything you've got.'

'That doesn't make sense.'

He held up the photo.

'Bunny, the girl in the photo …'

'Well?'

'It's me.'

Chapter 20

"I just feel so alone, even when I'm surrounded by other people."
Lost in Translation (2003)

The new cameras were aboard an army transporter. The word was they'd be arriving in Chiang Mai in ten minutes and be in Fang two hours later. OB was off doing something experimental in digital with Jensen while they still had him – while he was in the mood to perform. While everybody else waited, I took a stroll over to the area where the second camera crew was setting up beneath straw pavilions. Warriors, injured in battle: legs missing, intestines spilled, lay on bamboo stretchers playing drafts and telling jokes. They all seemed in good spirits for ones so mutilated. One minor Thai television celebrity sat in a pool of blood with an arrow entering his left eye and emerging from the back of his brain. He was arguing with his girlfriend on his cell phone.

'I told you, aluminium window frames work out a lot cheaper than wood in the long run.'

I caught sight of Thirayuth, Boon's head cameraman for the amok runners sequences. He was sitting on a dolly unit that would take him on a grizzly funfair ride between the litters. He looked uncomfortable on the small seat. He was a large untidy blob of a man – a Thai Michael Moore. If he'd done a day's exercise in his life it wouldn't have been long after nursery school. He recognized and obviously liked me.

'Hey stupid. Where have you been hiding out?' he asked.

'They made me a third-row, deep left wing comfort woman,' I said. 'I wasn't allowed to break rank until now.'

'Did they tell you if they ever get the cameras functioning you'll be trampled underfoot by a musk elephant before lunch? One of your own. Friendly fire.'

Thirayuth knew every scene in the movie. He'd had the shooting script translated, studied it and memorized the whole thing. Film was everything to him and he was born to it. He took it upon himself to understand every facet of the industry and dedicate his life to making perfect movies. Boon had pointed him out to me. 'This guy's going to be the biggest filmmaker in Asia.' He had the 'big' already.

'What are you doing?' I asked.

'Waiting. Waiting's what we do on a film set, Jimm. If I could have all those hours back that I've spent waiting I'd only be half the age I am now. Right now we're waiting for the US team to come down and check on us. We've been set up and ready for an hour but we can't film anything till we have permission. They don't trust us.'

We sat together at a picnic table and drank warm Coke.

'I'm sorry about what happened to Boon,' I said.

'Yeah, we all are. He should have been here doing this.'

'I don't understand it. Was anybody – I don't know, threatening him? Was he afraid of anything?'

'Hard to tell. He kept his feelings to himself mostly. He wouldn't want to upset anyone else with his own problems.'

'Your boys got any suspicions?'

'Suspicions? No.'

'Too bad.'

'We know who did it, though,' he said.

My eyes bulged. 'You do?'

'Sure. He told us he'd be missing the afternoon shoot on Friday cause he'd been summoned by the dog shits. That's what he called the cops. Dog-shit brown uniforms, you know?'

'He told you he had a meeting with the police?'

'Yeah.'

'Did you tell anyone this?' I asked.

'You mean, like the police?'

'What was the meeting about?'

'Money.'

'Damn.'

Sissy had befriended a group of extras. Or at least he'd managed to get as intimate as a man can with people who don't share his language. While they set up and tested the new cameras, OB walked Arny through the next scene. They only needed our brother's body as an approximation of Dan Jensen, currently playing Game Boy in his trailer. As they strolled around the set Sissy followed and gave his rendition of a Shan drinking song he'd learned from an old boyfriend. He had an ear for music and retained a vast repertoire of songs.

Had the extras actually been Shan, Sissy was certain one or two would have sung along with him. Either that or told him to stop butchering their song. They did neither. In fact, they showed no recognition of the song at all. So where did they come from? There were Shan living on both sides of the Thai border but the plantations and orchards of Fang were full of badly paid, poorly treated Shan workers who had fled the Burmese junta. If they were Thai Shan they'd know Thai. Their children, those who had been allowed citizenship, might attend Thai schools. To function in Thailand, at least one person in each community would be able to act as an interpreter with the authorities.

But, during the many water breaks, Sissy hit them with both Thai and English and they laughed and spoke amongst themselves but they obviously had no idea what he was saying. If they were acting dumb they were very good at it. They'd taken to this clown of a man who sang and laughed and spoke to them in tongues. Sissy even drew them pictures. With the aid of a pencil and the back of a script, He started to draw a map. He began with Fang. They recognized it. They also knew Chiang Mai and Hot near the border. Good, he was getting closer. He drew the Salaween River which divided Thailand from Burma. They nodded and laughed when he mimed a bad attempt at swimming across it.

He called on a magic communication finger, pointed it at one of the men and used it to transpose him from his circle in Fang to a spot on the map. Together with the word 'you' and an exaggerated shrug, it usually had the effect of getting a rough placement. In this case there was no such luck. The extra twirled his own finger in the air, brought it to rest on his naked knee and scratched it. The others laughed heartily. Obviously, geography wasn't his strong point. Sissy was about to try again when a shadow loomed over him like a bruise.

'They don't know.'

The newcomer's voice was as deep and unfriendly as shark infested mud. Sissy had seen him around. He was dressed as an extra although he stood a head taller than anyone else. This was the man Kuro had identified as the minder. He was a foreman, interpreting for assistant director Quirk and redirecting instructions to the men. He gave us the impression he would have been happier carrying a whip than a bull horn.

'They don't know what?' Sissy asked. He rose to his feet so as not to give the whip master the advantage but he still had to look up at him. The skin of the man's face was pulled back so tightly Sissy imagined an alligator clip behind his head holding the rest of it in place.

'Don't know what your map means. They're ignorant.'

'I was just asking…' Sissy began.

'They don't speak.'

'Yeah, I know. I was just …'

'They're all legal.'

'So I've heard. I was interested to find out where their villages are.'

'Come from everywhere.'

'Right. But just as an example, could you ask this gentleman where he was born?'

'Not my job. I translate for the movie people.' He leaned his taut face well into Sissy's space. 'Leave my men alone.'

It wouldn't have been that difficult to bounce up and butt him in the face at that range but probably not wise either. Instead, Sissy smiled.

'Sorry. Just trying to be friendly. See you, guys.'

He waved but they didn't wave back. Their heads were bowed and they stared at the grass. As he walked away he heard a volley of abuse from the foreman and he knew he'd touched a nerve.

Chapter 21

**"You ask how to fight an idea. I'll tell you how.
With another idea."**
Ben-Hur (1959)

In the lower-ground floor gallery of the Lamphun
Historical Museum were stone tablets and artefacts that
dated back to the tenth and eleventh centuries. Some of
the stoneware apparently came from an age before
centuries had numbers. But in the loft was a rarer
specimen. Burmese of origin, unfathomable to many,
Khin sat on a wooden box beneath the buzzing and
flickering light of a ceiling fluorescent tube. What little
meat there had been on her gangly frame had long
since been sweated away in that hot, windowless attic.

The proprietor, a haughty retired school head, had
been very reluctant to allow the Burmese access to her
precious palm leaf manuscripts. The letter from the
history department failed to impress her. She was
evidently familiar with Chiang Mai University. It wasn't
until Khin walked her through the stone tablet gallery
and translated three ancient texts with the ease of a
high school student reading grade-school primers that
she relented. She allowed the visitor two days, and the
manuscripts were absolutely not to be taken out of the
loft. She had presumably assumed Khin would be so
uncomfortable up there that she'd give up after a few
hours. But she didn't know Khin.

Every two hours she would climb down from her
steamy aerie, walk across the street to the Haripunchai
Temple, and buy ice and refreshments from the straw-
roofed shop in its grounds. With these and a crateful of

drinking water she was able to work through the night. If the unreasonable proprietor would only allow her two days, she would insist that they comprised of twenty-four hours apiece.

But it was at 11AM on the second day that the Burmese equivalent of the word 'eureka' was heard by one of the museum's rare visitors. This was a librarian from Nag's Head, North Carolina and she was probably unaccustomed to seeing dark-skinned women wrapped in a loin cloth descend from the ceiling. When Khin approached her she clearly teetered between running for her life and taking a photograph. But the mad woman was waving a sheet of paper and was so obviously filled with joy that she gave her the benefit of the doubt.

'My good madam,' said Khin.

'Well, hi there.'

'Yes. I would like to share with you this line which I have just translated from a very old text. It was in a manuscript which refers to the latter days of King Mangrai's reign.'

She paused and considered providing her with a context by summarizing Thai history. But she came to the conclusion that such a task might take more time than was allowed on the lady's tourist visa. Instead, she merely pointed out that Mangrai was the first of the Chiang Mai kings.

'Allow me,' said Khin.

'Go ahead. I'm all ears,' said the woman. She started adjusting her digital camera for interior portraits.

'Thank you. Here it goes.' She referred to her notes. "'... and King Mangrai would give much time and wealth to the betterment of the Pa Tan temple. As it was the farthest from the river, it was the most secure in times of flooding. Here it was he wrote his personal history and chose to see out his remaining spiritual years." Isn't that marvelous?'

'I must say you have such polished English,' said the woman.

'Thank you.'

'I'm serious. Could I trouble you to find the timer feature on my camera? I have so many problems with these new gadgets. My granddaughter bought it for me.'

'Yes. You wish to take a photograph?'

'Of the two of us, if you don't mind.'

'Very well. I shall go upstairs and put on some clothing.'

'Oh, no, dear. I want you just the way you are.'

'Really? Very well. Perhaps if I were to give you my address you'd be so kind as to send me a copy. This is a truly momentous day.'

'I can see that.'

Chapter 22

"Danger always strikes when everything seems fine."
Seven Samurai (1954)

Sissy hadn't spoken to me at all on the brief ride to the set. I deserved it. Once we'd arrived I hadn't been able to find him all day. We found ourselves at different locations on different schedules. We eventually met up at the house. Even before OB and the stars arrived the place was a hive. The evening security detail had swollen to four and there was now one extra housekeeper and a cook. A young girl was in the side garden hanging out clothes, presumably to be dried by the heat of the moon, and an elderly gentleman was tending the garden. I found Sissy on the balcony out of disguise. She'd unstrapped her chest and was wearing a Mumu and fluffy slippers.

'If it carries on like this, we're going to have to find a bigger place,' she said.

Good, she was talking to me.

'Want to go someplace else?'

'Good idea.'

We drove into the centre of Tha Ton without speaking and turned into the lane that would take us up to the Hollywood sign and the silvery pagoda on the mountain. Caribbeans negotiated hills with remarkable spunk which was just as well because some stretches of the road were perpendicular and the bends caught out even the most experienced drivers. The entire summit was a sprawling monastery. The monk's huts were neatly lined up with a karmic view of the town and the surrounding deforestation. The roads criss-crossed like strands of DNA but they all led to the same place - the brand spanking new pagoda at the summit. Although the spire was complete the interior was still undergoing work. Eleven standing stone Buddhas queued politely outside the back door awaiting admission.

Ours was the only vehicle in the stupa parking lot. We sat on a patch of grass in a spot that gave us a panoramic view of Tha Ton and the steep rolling hills all around it. The river threaded itself between them like a grubby bootlace. As the sun set, the mountains plunged sections of the town into shadow. It was as if the earth were getting itself settled; pulling up its blankets against the night.

'You know I'm sorry, don't you?' I said. 'The thing with Bunny.'

'You could have warned me,' said Sissy.

'There wasn't a chance when Arny wasn't there. He's fragile enough at the best of times. If he'd learned that Bunny was more interested in his transsexual brother than in him he'd never get over it.'

'Yeah, you're right.'

'Was it really awful?'

'Could have been worse. She's not talking to me.'

'How far did she get before ...?'

'Kiss on the cheek. And I saw her shaved bits.'

'Did she see yours?'

'No. I showed her a photo of Granddad Jah.'

'Well, that's enough to turn anyone off.'

We laughed and the chill was thawed. We shared our findings of the day and let those thoughts soak in as the scenery passed through various shades of sunset. Soon, only the lilac tiled spire behind us was tall enough to reflect light from the sinking sun.

'I wonder,' I said, 'if maybe the extra wasn't as bad at geography as you thought he was.'

'What do you mean?' Sissy asked.

'What if he pointed at his knee cause the map wasn't big enough? Cause where he comes from really was that far.'

'But that would mean he was from way up in the Shan states – deep in Burma.'

'Could be,' I said.

'You think the police here are involved in some kind of trafficking scheme?'

'The cops *are* immigration. It wouldn't be difficult.'

An electric light on a timer above the stupa entrance flicked to life behind us.

'If they were smuggling in illegals, wouldn't they keep quiet about it?' Sissy asked. 'They'd find them work tucked away on plantations and in factories. They wouldn't put them in a Hollywood movie, goddamn it.'

'Why not? The bigger the daring the less likely it is to be seen,' I said.

'Okay, we'll keep working on it.'

We walked past the queuing Buddhas on our way back to the jeep.

'Evening gentlemen,' said Sissy. 'The bathroom's free now.'

I gave them a high *wai* and muttered an apology on behalf of my sacrilegious brother. There was a crack like someone stepping on a dry branch. I felt a slash at the air in front of my face and heard a crunch. We both turned in time to see a bite-sized wound appear in the neck of the rear Buddha and watched his head nod and tumble to the ground.

We shouted at the same time, 'Get down!' and hit the dirt together.

'Over there, next hill,' I said.

'How do you know?'

'I felt the bullet pass my nose. That's the angle.'

A second bullet whistled over our heads.

'I'm not sure we're a hell of a lot safer down here,' I decided.

A third bullet – lower.

'He's getting his sights,' I said.

Without another word we scrambled on our bellies like commandos in the direction of the jeep. The Suzuki was parked at the top of the hill on a slope. Sissy had put a rock under the back wheel because the handbrake was just an ornament. We made it around to the far side of the jeep just as bullet four clanged into the front fender.

'Jesus, Jimm,' said Sissy. 'If he gets the gas tank or the tyres we'll be stuck up here.'

'Take the rock away,' I said.

'What?'

'The rock. Move it out from there. When she starts rolling we get in and stay low till we're out of range.'

'I'm not sure that's a great idea. It's facing the wrong direction and we're at the top of a mountain.'

A fifth bullet whistled just over the jeep. Against his better judgment, Sissy kicked the rock loose. I opened the driver's side door, took it out of gear and we gave a tug to start the Caribbean rolling.

'Get in,' I yelled. Sissy crawled over the seat and one more bullet shattered the passenger side wing mirror just above his head.

'Screw this.'

He threw himself flat on the driver's seat as the jeep slowly reversed itself down the hill. It picked up speed in no time.

'Sissy?' I screamed.

'Yeah?'

'Feel free to get up there and steer any time you like.'

'You get up there. There's a guy with a gun.'

'You're in the damn driving seat.'

The jeep was travelling fast now – scary fast. We were on a mountain, going backwards without a driver.

'Sissy!'

'Okay.'

He squirmed around, took hold of the wheel and poked his head up to glance through the windshield. The *chedi* was travelling away from us at a cracking pace. There was nothing but blackness in the rear mirror. He wrenched the wheel to the left and felt the jeep skid, tip onto two wheels then hover on its axis. It seemed to ponder whether or not to roll. He stamped on the brake and pushed up against his door. I threw myself across him. The vehicle shuddered then dropped bouncing onto its other two wheels.

Then settled.

'I don't usually let girls do that on the first date,' Sissy said as I looked up from his lap.

'We alive?' I asked.

We looked around. We were beyond the crest of the hill, safe from the sights of the sniper and miraculously safe from my brother's driving. He looked out of the side window at the drop. In daylight it was probably quite scenic. At this time of the evening it was like looking down from an airplane at a midnight ocean – or down the throat of death.

'Sissy?'

'Yeah?'

'Remember we used to sit on the deck at Khin's place and talk about how cool everything was. How people over in *farang*land would envy our peaceful lifestyle? How Nirvana had to be something like that deck on the side of Doi Suthep?'

'Yeah.'

When did we decide that wasn't good enough for us?'

Chapter 23

"Named must your fear be before banish it you can."
Star Wars; The Empire Strikes Back (1980)

We'd driven back to the house in silence. Sissy's hands had begun to shake on the wheel even before we reached the happy Chinese Buddha at the entrance to the temple. I'd taken over the driving. My hands were steadier but my stomach was knotted like a string of old Christmas lights. We both had plenty to consider.

Back at the house, Arny had gone to bed to rest his back. Bunny was in Bangkok for the night doing more blue-screen work. We joined Kuro on the balcony. He was trying to introduce us to Johnny Walker Blue. It was no more blue than Black was black or Red was red but it was exactly what we needed that night. The bank opposite seemed to present more of a threat than usual. The insects' dirge was more foreboding – a million noisy witnesses to our discomfort.

We'd settled down somewhat and the shakes had stopped by the time we heard the rotors of the helicopter that touched down on the cleared lot opposite the house. Once or twice a week, OB had taken to hitching a ride back to Chiang Mai with Dan Jensen. He liked to check the rushes in the studio of Living Films out on the Super Highway. He could have stayed at the Dhara Dhevi and come back with Jensen in the morning but he admitted there was only so much of the self-opined, whimpering little runt he could take. And OB had begun to treasure the nights on the balcony at the accountant's house. He liked being around people he didn't have to pretend with.

He stopped briefly at his room to get into shorts and a Biere Lao T-shirt and hurried out to the porch. I could imagine the words 'thank God' tattooed across his forehead. He stood at the rail and took in a lungful of nature. We gave him his minute's silence - the new ritual. When he was pure again, he turned to his housemates and smiled.

'Hi, OB,' we said.

'Gentlemen. Lady,' he smiled. 'What's our sin of choice for the evening?'

A glass was already waiting for him beside his recliner. He sat and sipped. He generally seemed to accept anything we put in front of him. Any sedative or stimulant would do him fine. If we passed around a penguin we were certain he'd chew on it quite contentedly. Once he was home he deferred all decision making to anybody else.

'Ah, Kuro,' he said. 'I see we're taking advantage of the absence of our starlet to do some serious man drinking. Do we tell dirty jokes and look at porn movies later, too?'

'Up to you,' Kuro said.

'You got any?' Sissy asked.

OB laughed too hysterically, too manically like a psychiatric patient letting go a trauma.

'What's happened?' I asked.

'We lost a can,' he said.

'Tuna?'

'Film. Today's shoots.'

'Everything?' Kuro asked.

'About two hours on the main camera.' He took a healthy slug of the light brown Blue and smiled. It was a particularly Thai smile.

'How? You've got security people,' I said.

'A whole team of 'em, yeah.'

'So, how …?'

'Somewhere between the helicopter landing spot and the studio. I don't know. John Quirk was with the cans the whole time. He gets a bit anal about not letting them out of his sight.'

'He had hold of them inside the helicopter, too?' I asked.

'Well, he wouldn't have been clutching them to his chest the whole way, but, yeah. I guess. Why?'

'It's a police helicopter, isn't it?'

'Yes, it is. Do you know something, Jimm?'

During our drive back to the house, we'd decided it was time to share our fears with as many people as possible. There was nothing heroic in dying with a secret. We dragged Arny out of his early bed and huddled together on the balcony, the drinks forgotten. Sissy acted as narrator: the attempts on our lives, the connection with director Boon, and finally the mystery of the non-Shan-speaking Shan. And he was careful to keep pulling on the thread that ran through it all – the Fang police.

'Hell!' said OB. He topped up his glass and drank half.

Kuro smiled in a way that some clever westerners describe as 'inscrutable' but which is actually just the Japanese way of saying, 'Shit!'

'Okay,' OB sat nodding through his thoughts. 'Then let's suppose all these unfortunate accidents we're having on and around the set aren't accidents at all.'

I sat up and counted them off on my fingers. 'Two bush fires in two days. Two rocket-proof cameras breaking down at the same time. Extras retreating despite very clear instructions they should be attacking. A lost can of film. I don't know. That doesn't take much supposing in my book.'

'All right then,' OB nodded. 'So what do they hope to gain? They were delighted to have us here. The police major and the governor gave a dinner in our honour. They told us how hard they'd fought to have this movie shot in their district. It meant extra income for Fang retailers and hoteliers. Why would they want to sabotage the whole thing?'

We sat quietly pondering that very point.

'I get a feeling we've got all the parts but we aren't putting them together right,' I said.

'I agree,' said Sissy. 'And I've got a hunch if we can find out what the story is with those extras we'll be half way to seeing the picture. OB, what do you know about their work permits and visas?'

'I can check.'

I nodded. 'I doubt we'll come up with anything there. But it'll help to know just what documents these guys need to work here. Are they all legal? That kind of thing. I just have this feeling there's something bigger. We really should talk to the extras without their minder breathing down our necks.'

Kuro ran his hand through his long black hair, frowned like Toshiro Mifune, and sucked in a tight hiss like the door closing on an airport shuttle bus. I could imagine a million teenage boys in Japan standing in front of a mirror and practicing that self-same gesture.

'The probrem is,' he said. 'we don't know what ranguage they speak.'

'What we could do is record them while they're together and have someone analyze it,' OB suggested.

I looked at Sissy. A different idea had occurred to us simultaneously.

'Better than that,' I said. 'We bring in someone who can go straight into the interview.'

Chapter 24

"Alone, bad. Friend, good."
Bride of Frankenstein(1935)

Khin was at the west wall of Wieng Kum Kam pacing. She wore an enormous straw hat and when she stood still to record her measurements she looked like a well-used beach umbrella. Her footprints criss-crossed the entire area. The residents whose houses backed on to the site had been watching her through their kitchen windows, wondering when she'd faint from the heat. But they didn't know Khin.

'Anyone mentioned you look like a sun flower in that hat?' I said.

Khin turned to the voice and saw me leaning on a sacred boundary marker as if it were a pile of bricks.

'Jimm,' said Khin enthusiastically. 'Delighted to see you.' She came over and shook my hand. 'And your film?'

'I took the day off.'

Khin's countenance became overcast with the threat of rain.

'Oh dear. I promised to telephone you to inform you of my progress, didn't I? I have been a recalcitrant member of the amok runners. I have been plunged into a frenzied period of confounding activity, you see? Forgive me.'

'You're forgiven. All I know is you're a pain in the ass to find.'

'Yes. Then, how did you succeed?'

'Last thing we knew you were at the museum in Lamphun.'

'You went there?'

'Yeah. And the watchman said you'd left there happy as a finch and not told a soul where you were off to. So, I figured, if you were in that good a mood you probably weren't on your way back to Burma. You must have found something to support this month's Mangrai theory. And that's what brought me here. I asked a few people if they'd seen a skinny Burmese prodding and probing around the sites and step by step they pointed me in this direction.'

'Brilliant,' she said. 'You should have been a detective rather than a hack.'

'I'm a reporter, Khin.'

'Same difference. But why have you been so diligent in your search for me, Jimm?'

'We need you.'

'I am touched. What for?'

'It's a long story. Is there somewhere we can sit and talk out of the sun?'

'Certainly. There is my house.'

'Your ...? You have a house?'

'I used the American aid money to rent a domicile.'

'Where?'

'Right here in Wieng Kum Kam. At the heart of my place of employment you might say.'

Khin walked me through the narrow streets of little houses, all of which seemed to resent the presence of the ancient ruins in their community. Nobody wanted a heap of rubble as a next door neighbour, not even the poorest householder. We passed a toy town-sized shop whose old lady proprietor seemed to have been scaled down to fit her establishment.

'Hello, teacher,' she said in English.

'Hello, Mrs. Lah,' said Khin.

'Looks like you rule the hood already, Khin,' I said.

'That was my local Seven-Eleven,' she blushed. 'And this …' She held out her hand like a game-show hostess pointing to the night's star prize, 'this is my abode.'

It was the sorriest looking hovel I'd seen in a while – low and bare, like a concrete gun placement on some windswept coast. It was scarcely broad enough for a woman of Khin's height to lay lengthwise without banging her head against the wall. It was sky blue and apparently suffering from earthquake damage. We entered but neither of us bothered to take off our shoes. There was no optical illusion. It didn't magically defy dimensions and turn into a vast chamber inside. The ceiling was low enough to touch and it was basically one room – the living, sleeping, dining area and a kitchen alcove. The bathroom, toilet, spa, Jacuzzi was in a packing case-sized construction in the back yard.

'So,' I asked, already sensing the worst, 'how much are you paying for this?'

'Yes. It was a steal, Jimm. Only eight thousand *baht* a month – and a mere two months down payment.'

'That really is a steal, Khin,' I said.

'And they didn't even ask to see my particulars.'

'You surprise me. And they'll be shipping in the furniture when?'

'The mattress is more than adequate. Although I confess a refrigerator might not come amiss.'

She seemed so happy I didn't have the heart to shoot her down. A change of subject was in order. There were no chairs upon which to sit nor table upon which to lean, so we sat cross-legged on the mattress. I began to itch as soon as I lowered myself onto it.

'Khin, my sister.'

'Yes?'

'We have a mission.'

'I see.'

'I need you to come back to Fang with me.'

The pallor of disappointment passed across Khin's face quickly like the shadow of a 747. I knew the poor woman was being wrenched from the love of her life but the Burmese sense of honour amongst friends outweighed her frustration. I was also aware that Khin's love affair would never be requited and a few days off might actually do her good.

'Your wish is my command,' said Khin.

'It shouldn't take long.'

'Tell me of your problem.'

As I told the tale and described what role we hoped Khin might play, I noticed a non-dripping tear form in the corner of my friend's eye. Khin inflated with pride right there in front of me. I believed if the Burmese had been in possession of cutlery she might have gone so far as to make an incision in our two palms and swear a blood allegiance right there on the living room floor.

'I don't know how to repay you for this opportunity,' Khin said, leaving me stuck for a response. It was clear that Khin saw this as a way, in small part, of repaying the mountain of kindnesses she'd received since we adopted her.

'No, in fact I do,' she decided. 'When everything is resolved in Fang, Sissy and Arny and yourself will come here as my guests ...'

'Khin, that really isn't necess ...'

'... and together we shall ...'

'Khin.'

'Together we shall recover the great treasure of King Mangrai. It is the least I can do. I insist.'

I puffed out my cheeks and turned to look into the delighted, childlike face of Khin of Burma.

'Thanks, Khin.'

Chapter 25

"Nobody takes a picture of something they want to forget."
One Hour Photo (2002)

Despite all he'd learned about the Fang police, OB had a movie to make. He'd urged us to abandon our mission and return to Chiang Mai, but it didn't surprise him when we refused. There was something of the mild-mannered super hero in him too. He wanted to avenge those who had suffered and climb tall buildings in the pursuit of justice. That undying belief that we were more righteous than our foe reminded OB of his fiery youth – of the boy who'd made documentaries that told the truth. In those days the truth had been a dangerous weapon. He'd taken on the corporations and the establishment and he'd made dents. You could never completely crush the bastards but there had been battles won and faces broken. The pledge of allegiance we'd made on the Saturday evening had been particularly Fantastic Four-like.

Over the years, OB had gazed down upon a sea of flesh from his scaffold. Like most directors he had stopped seeing the bit players as people. They were scenery with legs. But today there was a new dimension to the game. He visualized, not only the effect the movement of the extras would produce on screen, but also the drama that might be playing on their lives. What intrigue was afoot? For the first time in many decades the fact had become more important to him than the fantasy. It occurred to him that distracting people from reality wasn't nearly as satisfying as changing the reality itself.

They were reshooting the lost can. The extras in Thai garb charged and charged again, all give or take those who retreated. In post-production the army would become two-hundred thousand. Twenty-first century audiences hummed at two-thousand. In the Rings series, Jackson had conjured militias of a million. In Troy a fleet of a hundred thousand ships was already a thing of no great wonder. Hollywood had become a slave to excess.

There was an observer zone at the shoot sight. It kept all the visitors in one spot so there would be less likelihood of some actor's mother strolling across a battle scene with a video camera. Local dignitaries and the press were fenced off in this compound and shepherded by an official with a walky-talky. They were situated on the top of a hill and had refreshments and clean Porta-johns to keep everything civilized. From this vantage point one could see the corner of the city walls and the palace in the distance. There was a good view of the camera placements and the largely unemployed extras and elephants. And high on his metal throne sat the great director passing on judgments electronically.

Major Ketthai and Sergeant Manuth stood in the observer zone with police-issue binoculars. The major was giving orientation to his new sergeant following the sad and sudden death of his predecessor. They were not watching the coordination of the men down in the valley but instead trained their glasses on the back of their new target.

'That one,' said Ketthai. 'Do you see him?'

'The old one? Yes major. I see him.'

'They call him OB. The actors have bodyguards but this one thinks he's special. I don't want any mistakes, understand?'

'Yes, sir.'

Manuth still had the hop, skip and salivary glands of a puppy dog. He was eager to please the major. But Ketthai despaired at the lower ranks – so enthusiastic to work their way into the upper circle where the serious money was to be made, but so incompetent. And now the academy was talking about honour and honesty there seemed little hope of finding young police officers with the right attitude any more. But, he had to give this one his due. He'd handled the dispatch of Sergeant Chat most competently. Chat had taken to drinking and talking too much about the wrong things. He was careless. He'd bungled the shooting and setting up the dead body. He'd been due an accident and his replacement arranged it well. Perhaps there was hope.

Chapter 26

"If there's anything in the world I hate, it's leeches - oh, the filthy little devils!"
The African Queen (1951)

Sissy walked along the air-conditioned hallway and admired the artfully framed portrait photographs of Thai celebrities he couldn't name. He was a television amputee. He knew nothing about Thai pop culture and had no ambition to learn. Life was too short and fame too fleeting to invest time on its study. He'd given Thai cinema its chance and there were flowers blooming here and there but mostly it was a desert of schlocky horror and whacky slapstick. Directors gave the audiences what they were used to and didn't feel obliged to wean them off the sugary diet they'd been on for generations.

Ask Sissy about Thai literature and art and he'd hold his own in sophisticated company but the average eight-year-old could out-pop him hands down. The faces that watched his progress through the studio corridors were air-brushed strangers; too young to be talented, too pretty to be permanent. He used to be one of those pretties so he knew. This day he was more elegant than glamorous in a beige skirt suit and high heels. He'd applied his makeup in the airplane so it wasn't perfect but it would do. He turned a corner as the receptionist had instructed and came face to limited-feature-face with Gus.

'Oh, good,' Sissy said.

'Fuck you want?' he said.

Sissy was surprised he recognized him.

'I'm good, thanks. You?'

'I said, the fuck do you want?'

'All grammar aside, I have an appointment with Ms Savage,' Sissy told him.

Gus was standing sentry in front of the door marked *bluescreen studio*. It was a double door but he had it covered. He looked my brother up and down, snorted then managed the longest stream of dialogue Sissy had heard from him since they'd first become buddies.

'You're a loser,' he said in a gravelly whisper. 'And I personally don't see what Miss Savage sees in you. You think dressing up like a girl's gonna impress her? Make you different from the others? I know bums like you and I know what you're after. You make my job difficult. So why don't you get lost?'

The igloo had been hired for traits other than his good looks and repartee but Sissy admired a man who spoke his mind.

'Come on, pal,' said Sissy and made a show of clicking his neck. 'We don't have to be enemies. You know who I am and …'

'I know you're good for nothing, is all I know. I know you're a dope-head and an opportunist.'

Sissy was surprised Gus knew a word like opportunist. Perhaps they were both misreading each other.

'Does that mean you aren't going to let me in?'

'You're not on my list.'

Sissy saw neither a list nor an attempt to look for one.

'Gus, my friend. You clearly have a dilemma here. I'm the current best friend of the woman who employs you.'

Gus tensed all his muscles at once and probably caused a tsunami off Hong Kong.

'I know that pisses you off,' Sissy continued, 'but them's the marbles. So over afternoon tea I lean across to my best friend and suggest that she replaces you with someone blacker and nicer. Miss Savage will say, 'Well sure, Sissy. Whatever you say,' and you, Gus, will be watching *Home Alone 6* in economy on your way back to the states. So, here's where we are. You either get it out of your system and beat me to wasabe right here and now or you get over it and continue to earn your two thousand bucks a day. Up to you. Just don't forget; you're her minder, not her father.'

Sissy detected some kind of vibration the length and breadth of Gus. He rocked from side to side. All those conflicting urges - *get rich, kill, get rich, kill* - seemed to be running through his veins. Then, like a spin drier at the end of its cycle, he reached a still calm and stood to one side.

The large studio was in shadow all but the blue light stage. It engulfed Bunny Savage on three sides like a heavy sky. She was dressed in her Shan princess go-go gear and held a sword. If it had been made of anything but balsa it would have weighed more than she did. A voice that boomed around the high-ceilinged studio was giving her instructions.

'Okay. There's a damned enormous chariot coming up behind you. You hear it first, look surprised. Look over your left shoulder and there it is. Run and roll.'

Sissy didn't see a chariot but Bunny evidently did. There was a consummate look of terror on her face as she strove to avoid its spiked wheels. She was a very good actress if she could fake a Burmese chariot. He sat at the back of the room watching her act. She spent another hour avoiding death from a variety of threats. It appeared to Sissy that the life of a Shan princess was a particularly hazardous one. He looked around at the crew. They were drooling, fantasizing, acting as cute and interesting as they possibly could. The star, glistening with sweat, glowing with sexuality, took a while to realize who the elegant woman in stilettos was. But, to give her credit, she smiled, walked up to Sissy and gave him a kiss on the cheek.

'My lover woman,' she said.

'You've forgiven me?'

'It was all me being dumb. You're innocent. What are you doing here?'

'I have to talk to a casting company.'

'Ooh, all the excitement of the movie business gone to your head? Did you look at Jensen and decide, if he can do it …?'

'No, well … yeah. I do think that. But that's not the reason. Can we go somewhere and talk?'

She had a suite at the Intercontinental. They drank freshly-squeezed mango juice and sat on the Jim Thomson silk-covered sofa, her legs on the coffee table.

'Why didn't you tell me any of this before?' she asked.

'I was being manly.'

'Perhaps a bit too manly,' she said. 'Protecting the fragile maiden from the truth?'

'Something like that.'

'So, why are you telling me now?'

'We decided the more people that know the better. They'd have to kill the whole lot of you to keep their secrets.'

'But it looks like you don't know what their secrets are.'

'They obviously think we do.'

'And how does this casting agency fit in?'

'Star Casting and Locations. It's the firm OB's people had originally been recommended. It was a big contract. They had to help with the location scouting and find Thai actors to play the smaller roles and line up extras. But at the last minute they decided they weren't up to it. They handed the whole contract over to some little outfit called Northern Thai Casting. Nobody's ever heard of them. The only number Star had was a cell phone.'

'And nobody's answering,' she guessed.

'You got it.'

'So, you've got an appointment to meet the head of the company.'

'Nope.'

'Why not?'

'Because I'm a part-time computer geek from Chiang Mai.'

'So, then … oh, I see.'

He took his cell from his handbag, found the number and handed it to her.

'Thanks,' he said.

'I feel so used.'

The head of Star Casting was four feet seven and built like a bag of rice. She had short reddish hair gelled vertical and a nose ring. She wore sparkly jeans and a black velvet jacket with the sleeves rolled to her elbows. Unlike Sissy, she'd left the country to acquire her American accent. Sissy had checked the company website and discovered Star Casting's CEO had spent fifteen years in San Francisco.

'Hi, I'm Tip,' she said, when Bunny Savage opened the door. The woman held up a bottle wrapped in shiny gold paper. 'It's not much, but I didn't have a lot of notice to go shopping.'

'Hello, Tip,' said Bunny. 'Come in, please. I hope you don't mind eating up here.'

'It's never gonna happen to me but I imagine getting ogled in public places would get old real fast,' she said.

Tip was obviously nervous and excited. She hopped from foot to foot and banged her fists together in front of her. Bunny pointed to the set table.

'Won't you sit down?'

She saw Tip look at the third placement but not make a comment.

'I have to say I was shocked to get your call. I'm a big fan. I mean a *big* fan.'

'That's sweet.'

'I can't believe you knew Malee in California. She never mentioned it. I mean,' Tip continued, 'I'm sorry I was cold on the phone. I just didn't believe it was you. I was mad at my secretary for being so easily taken in. Then it turned out it was really you. This is great. I'm so excited. I can dine out on this for months.'

Sissy appeared from the other room and Tip got to her feet.

'This is my friend, Sissy,' Bunny said.

'Hi.'

'Hi.'

Sissy sat across the table from her. She must have felt obliged to keep talking.

'So, how do you know Malee?'

Bunny joined them at the table, took the champagne bottle from the bucket and poured for Tip and Sissy.

'I don't,' she said.

'I'm sorry?'

'I don't know Malee. I lied.'

Bunny didn't know anybody called Malee in California or anywhere else for that matter. It was a ruse devised by Sissy to get Tip there to the hotel. It began with the phone call and the line, 'Hi, this is Bunny Savage. I'm in Thailand shooting a movie and I promised a mutual friend of ours I'd look you up.' This was followed by a long silence after which, hopefully Tip would say, 'Not Malee?' or some such name. It worked more often than not. Sissy had used it in his old life.

'Wh ... I don't understand,' said Tip.

Sissy took up the story. 'It was a little dishonest but it did get you here.'

Tip smiled to cover her discomfort.

'We want to talk to you about why you passed up the Siam contract.'

Any remaining sincerity drained from Tip's smile. The girlish fan morphed into the officious head of a large company. Her eyes hooded. Her voice deepened.

'There was no *Siam* contract. And what gives you the ...?

'There was,' Sissy said bluntly. 'You gave it away.'

Tip stood up.

'Things like that happen in business.'

'Only in funny business.'

Still holding onto her meaningless smile Tip stepped away from the table. 'If I'd known this was an official meeting I'd have sent one of my staff. I don't appreciate being duped.'

Bunny put her elbows on the table and rested her chin on a raft of fingers.

'Tip, did you happen to notice a big square guy in front of the door when you came in?'

She didn't reply.

'He's there for two reasons: to stop people getting in and to stop them getting out. He's in 'out' mode at the moment.'

'You think you can …? What is this all about?'

She took her cell phone from her pocket and held it in front of her like a weapon, her finger poised over the fast dial button.

'In Fang, there have been attempts on our lives,' Sissy told her. 'We aren't a threat to you. We just want to know what it's all about so we can stop any more violence. They killed Director Pongpun. All we want is your attention and a little chat. If we can get that in an amicable way it would be much better.'

'Amicable? You drag me here under false pretences then tell me I can't leave?'

'I know', said Sissy. 'Damned rude. And we should be ashamed of ourselves. But, trust me, the things we want to talk about are very relevant to you and the future and reputation of your company. You can press your speed dial and shout for help if you want, but then it'll come as even more of a shock when you find yourself unemployed and bankrupt.'

'And in jail,' Bunny added. 'Sit down and have a sip of champagne. It's Cristal. Too good to throw down the sink. Come on.'

Tip put her phone in her pocket and grabbed hold of the back of the chair as if her legs were about to give way. She looked at the vanilla white ceiling above her and a gang of emotions seemed to invade her face. After a deep breath she lowered herself onto the seat.

'We're working on the movie in Tha Ton,' Sissy continued. 'After the first week, Pongpun Wichaiwong was shot to death in a parking lot in Chiang Mai. A few days later a bomber attempted to blow me and my family to high heaven. Two nights ago we were shot at. The filming has been sabotaged at least three times and there are a couple of thousand extras sitting around and none of them speaks Thai.'

Tip sat staring at the bubbles milling in the glass. Sissy had her attention.

'Now, in San Francisco you'd go see the police and get them to sort everything out for you,' he said. 'But we have a strong suspicion that if the police *weren't* involved we wouldn't be having any of these problems. As it was you that passed this project on to the mysterious Northern Thai Castings, which, by the way, seems to have been liquidated as soon as the deals were done, I'd say your company is in deep shit. I'd say you'll probably never get another overseas contract. So it might help all parties concerned if you'd be so kind as to share with us exactly why you passed this deal on to a bunch of crooks.'

He was surprised to see tears dribbling down Tip's face. He immediately felt like a bully and wanted to apologize but it was clear she needed to talk. Bunny slid her chair across and put an arm around the little CEO. They had to wait several minutes before the sobs subsided. The only emotion on Tip's face now was unhidden grief. Bunny handed her a napkin and she wiped away the tears.

'Somjit went to the north with the location scout from LA,' she began. 'Somjit is my partner – in the company – we started it together – and in life. We've been together for twenty years. She liked to do the field work and see parts of the country you wouldn't normally get a chance to see if you're stuck in an office in Bangkok. The American was interested in Fang, particularly around Tha Ton. So they went to see the local authorities there and everything seemed to be cool for everyone.

'Somjit came back and agreed terms with the movie people and we signed a contract. We even started casting for the bigger roles. She made another trip up north to take photos of spots around Chiang Mai and talk to the people running the elephant camps. We were supposed to find two hundred elephants from someplace. And she ...'

Tip's voice suddenly became dry and throaty. She emptied the glass of champagne without bothering to enjoy it.

'She disappeared,' Tip went on. 'One night she didn't call. It was our habit to talk on the phone every evening at six. I assumed she was stuck in a meeting or on the road. I called her cell but the message said it was out of service. It was weird. She always had her phone with her, always kept it charged. So I thought perhaps she's in a place with no signal. Next day, no call. She didn't reply to emails, nothing. Of course I was worried.

'The problem was I didn't know exactly where she was. Last time we spoke she was in Chiang Mai and said she'd be working her way up to Fang – stopping off at the camps. When I called the police, I couldn't tell them where she might have been. They said, 'She'll turn up.' She didn't. We went up there, me and two staff. Went to all the camps, resorts, hotels. We asked. Searched. Nothing. I even hired a guy. We'd used him before. He was a sort of private investigator. He had contacts. The last place anyone saw Somjit was at the elephant show grounds in Chiang Dao but whether she'd carried on north from there or turned back to the city, nobody knew.

'I was shattered. Couldn't sleep. Didn't know what to do – who to turn to. I had to come back to the company but I had the guy in the north stay on it full time. It was like … I don't know. Like she just dissolved.'

Bunny refilled Tip's glass and she finished that also.

'I was working late one night,' she continued. 'That was my life then – work. And the security guard called up to my office. He told me there were some men downstairs from Fang with urgent news. I buzzed them up. There were these two – short hair – shifty looking. I felt … I don't know, exposed, vulnerable. I couldn't understand why the security guard stayed downstairs. I wished he hadn't let them in.

'They were, what's the word? Condescending. Asked how someone like me could operate a company. Asked if my dad allowed me to make decisions. I didn't know how to talk to them. They said they were from a company in Chiang Mai called Northern Thai Castings. I said I'd never heard of it. They said there was a Hollywood movie coming to Fang and the local authorities had decided, as it was a northern production they didn't want a Bangkok company handling it.

'I laughed and one of them slapped my face, made my nose bleed. The other one pushed me back into my chair and yanked out the phone. I pressed the alarm button under my desk. It was supposed to bring the security people running but nothing happened. He said, "maybe you don't understand" and pulled a wad of documents from his briefcase. On top was a contract; three copies. It signed over the rights for casting and location for *Siam* to Northern Thai. I refused to sign. I told them times had changed in Thailand. We didn't do business like that anymore. He slapped me again. But I wasn't going to sign anything.

'Where were the security people? I had no idea what to do. I told them, even if I wanted to – and I didn't – I couldn't sign any documents. All contracts had to be co-signed by both directors and witnessed for them to mean anything. He flipped the papers to the back page and my heart just died. It was Somjit's signature on all three copies. I couldn't imagine what had possessed her to … I asked where she was – what had they done with her? Then they showed me the photograph – just the one, and I stopped living, I swear. I was numb for a minute. I couldn't bring myself to react. I can't bear to think about it. She looked so … so empty of hope. She was cut, bruised. Her eyes were looking off into some far off place. I wanted to rip their throats out, those two …'

Tip broke down again and allowed Bunny to squeeze an arm around her. She and Sissy were crying too – tears free-flowing. The pain was almost vented. The poor woman had just one more lap to go and all the hate and misery she'd bottled up would be out. Not better, but shared.

'They told me it was a simple business deal', she said. 'I sign over the Siam contract and I get back my partner. Did I believe them? Did I honestly think they'd honour the deal and send her back from hell? No. I told them – I was shaking, I was peeing my pants, but I had to try. I told them to bring her to me unharmed and when I saw she was alive I'd sign. The same man who'd shown me the photo took a sheet from his bag and put it on the desk in front of me. It was a list of names and locations. At the top was an address I knew very well. It was the house I'd grown up in. The house where my parents still live. All my friends and family were on the list. He said, 'How do you think we got your girlfriend to sign?'

'Once I'd put my signature on the contracts he came and sat in front of me on the desk. He reached into his back pocket and took out his wallet. He said "If I were you I'd go to the police about this violation of your rights. You'd be quite justified and I'd respect you for it. There's only one small problem." He took out one card and held it in front of me. His thumb was over the name but I got to see the rest of it. It was a Royal Thai Police identification card with his photo.

'He said, "We're here night and day to protect our Thai brothers and sisters. Just give us a call. Word would get to us almost straight away." And before they left, the other one looked back and smiled. "We've still got her. The boys have taken a liking to her, if you know what I mean."

'What could I do?

What could I do?'

Chapter 27

"Truth hurts. Maybe not as much as jumping on a bicycle with the seat missing, but it hurts."
The Naked Gun 2½ (1991)

That night, Sissy looked up an old friend. He'd always had a thing for men in uniform but recent events had made him wary. The meeting had gone on till the early hours and only time would tell as to whether he'd made a serious error of judgment. It wouldn't have been the first time. He'd gone directly to the airport and met up with Bunny and adorable Gus. They'd taken the 6:30 Thai Airways flight to Chiang Mai, first class on Bunny's credit card. Sissy had never travelled first class on a fifty minute flight before and he didn't really have much of an opportunity to appreciate it.

They ate a speedy breakfast and following the new policy of sharing information with as many people as possible Bunny told Gus all about the subterfuge in Fang. They didn't expect him to have any insights or even to understand it all but if they needed his bulk for stopping bullets at least he'd know to stand facing the police rather than behind them.

They reached the Swiss accountant's house by eleven. Khin was there to meet them. She'd arrived on the eight o'clock bus. OB and Kuro had left for the shoot much earlier but there was a note attached to Sissy's pillow.

'Calling a meeting of the troops at lunch time. My trailer. New info. OB.'

They drove out to the site in the Lexus. They'd been expecting the place to be rocking with activity. The air was comparatively clear and the new cameras were behaving splendidly. So it surprised them to see everyone sitting around locked into a state of ennui. As they left the car they wondered what new disaster had lit upon Siam this day.

Gus escorted Bunny to her trailer and Sissy and Khin went off in search of me. They found Arny and me in dialogue with Kuro passing on the information Sissy had phoned through the previous night.

'Hi, guys,' said Sissy.

'Did you stop off at the house?' I asked.

'Yeah.'

'I guess you didn't see OB?'

'No. He'd left a note. Why? What's happened?'

'He and his car did not arrive here,' Kuro told him. 'He reft thirty minutes before me. I don't see him broke down on the road but when I come – he is not here. He does not answer the phone.'

'Oh, shit,' said Sissy. 'What are we doing about it?'

'His gofer called the cops,' said Arny.

'Gr-eat!'

'They got here faster than the speed of light. The major himself was up here strutting around.'

'I bet he was,' said Sissy. 'Oh, man. I hope they haven't done anything to OB.'

'We cannot understand this at all, Sissy San,' said Kuro, running his hand through his hair. 'We cannot work out what is the benefit of stopping this movie. And what is the advantage to murder international cerebrity?'

'None at all as far as I can see,' Sissy decided. 'But that just means we haven't got the first damned idea what's going on here.'

'Khin, my sister,' I said.

'Yes?'

'What do you say you, me and Arny go chat with some mysterious extras?'

'Lead the way, mistress.'

'And we'll see you two at OB's trailer at twelve just in case he got himself lost deliberately.'

The secret of getting the extras into a space and mood where they could speak freely was to locate the foreman then pick out stragglers at the other side of the herd so he couldn't see. We found the tall man at the administration tent filling in forms and immediately picked our way through the idle non-Shan almost to the edge of the city wall.

'They are most certainly Wa speakers,' said Khin.

'You worked that out without talking to anyone?' Arny asked.

'I have ears, young man. I have picked up enough to know. The Wa language is very different from any other. It has Khmer origins. The Wa people have been forcibly relocated from the north of Burma by the junta in order to work the land.'

'You think they're in this country illegally?'

'Indubitably. I cannot for one second imagine two thousand Wa securing temporary work permits. Given their background in opium production I imagine the American embassy would nix such an arrangement.'

'Can you speak to them?' Arny asked.

'At a rudimentary level.'

'Cool. Then we have to make friends with one or two.'

'If I may beg to differ, I'd like to suggest a more plausible alternative,' said Khin.

'Shoot,' I said.

'Despite their relaxed attitude at present, I am getting a subliminal feeling that these chaps are not entirely confident about being on foreign soil without documentation. I would be terribly surprised if we could enter into an enduring friendship based on a ten minute conversation.'

'What do you have in mind?'

'Bullying.'

'You sure?' asked Arny.

'It is the tried and tested Burmese method of extracting information from minorities. They expect it of us.'

'Then go ahead,' I told her.

'Thank you.'

We found a timid-looking middle-aged archer readjusting his uniform as he returned from the tree line. Like most of the extras, he'd ignored the well-equipped but claustrophobic Porta-johns and done his business in the bushes. This soldier was a sun-blackened man with a fine head of hair but Khin identified something subjugable about him. The man lowered his head as we approached.

Khin barked at him and he mumbled a response. I was impressed. The Burmese had risen to her full height and thrown forward a chest that I couldn't recall having seen before. Khin had clearly been a very keen student of military oppression. She marched the little man around the polystyrene edge of the city wall and found a nook. She ordered him to stand at ease with his back to the parapet while she prowled back and forth like an over-acting Gestapo officer. The poor Wa trembled.

'Steady Khin,' I warned. 'We don't want him having a heart attack before we get anything out of him.'

'Plenty more where this came from,' she said. 'Should I kick him?'

'Khin!'

'Yes, I'm sorry. What do you need to know?'

But before Khin could ask, the man blurted out a rapid stream of uninvited dialogue.

'What's he saying?'

'It's a little fast but the gist is that he wants us to know why he didn't use the plastic water closet as he'd been instructed.'

I kept my face straight. 'Tell him he's in a lot more trouble than shitting in the woods.'

Khin obliged.

'And tell him I'm from the immigration department and I know he's planning to migrate to Thailand illegally.'

Khin managed to stretch that one sentence into ten. When the point was finally made the little man reacted strongly. He had a lot to say and it was all Khin could do to put the brakes on him. The Wa was obviously nervous. To my uneducated ears it appeared a whole cauldron of beans was in the process of being spilled. With a little clarification here and there from his interrogator the man finally reached the end of his defence. Khin nodded and turned to us.

'And there we have it.'

'What do we have, Khin?' Arny asked.

'It would appear that neither he nor his brothers have any interest or ambition to stay here beyond the duration of the film. They were coerced by an agent of the United Wa State Army on the Burmese side who told them they'd be sent to Thailand to do two weeks 'legal' work for which they'd be recompensed. They were ferried to the border. Everything was cleared by the border patrol and Thai Immigration.'

'A.K.A the Fang police,' I said.

'Precisely. Most of the extras have family back in the Wa relocation zone and humble farms to go back to. With Burmese troops around it is particularly dangerous to leave ones wife and daughters unattended, if you know what I mean. They are afraid their family would suffer if they failed to go home. And believe me, the Wa already know a good deal about suffering.'

'So, it's not about trafficking.'

'It would appear not.'

'So how…?' And then it came to me. I slapped myself on the forehead so loud they probably heard it back in Tha Ton. 'Oh, man!'

'You are having some kind of brainstorm?' Khin asked.

'I should have known better,' I said. 'This is a police scam, Khin. There we were trying to turn it into something brilliant – some complicated mystery.'

'But it's not?'

'I've been so stupid. I need you to ask him just one more question but I think I already know what the answer's going to be.'

Chapter 28

"What is ten times a thousand?"
The Full Monty (1997)

Sissy and Kuro and Bunny Savage were sitting around the comfortable lounge area in OB's trailer. Lizzie the gofer was back from an unsuccessful search of the area. Through an interpreter she'd received a very calm, 'Don't worry. This will all be resolved,' from the police major.

'I called the embassy,' she said. She was speaking at neat-coffee speed. 'They're sending up some of their security people. They've contacted the government. Oh my God. This is a disaster. How could something like this happen?'

We arrived at the open door in time to hear her squeeze out four more clichés. We climbed up the steps and sat together on the sofa. I winked at Sissy with a broad, self-satisfied smile on my face. When Lizzie allowed a very brief gap in her stream of anxiety I took the opportunity to jump in.

'He'll be back,' I said.

'She turned to him, 'What?'

'OB – he'll be back.'

'You've heard from him?'

'Nope.'

'Then how could you know?'

'It's a hunch.'

'Oh, great. Then we can all rest easy,' she said, pacing again. 'There's a psychic in the house.'

Bunny crossed the trailer and wedged herself between me and Sissy on the sofa. She looked up at the gofer who was wearing a groove in the trailer floor.

'Lizzie, babe. Take an angst break. I want to hear what my girl here has to say for herself.'

'Me too,' the samurai king agreed.

'Okay, let's hear it,' Lizzie stood with her hands on her waist. 'When can we expect the boss back?'

'Ooh, I'd say mid-afternoon,' I said. 'Early evening at the latest.'

'And this is based on …?'

'Like I say, it's a hunch. But it's an intelligent one. It's based on the fact that whoever's scuttling this production isn't trying to close it down. In fact they're doing everything they can to make it last as long as possible.'

'How so?' Sissy asked.

'Well, look at the fires,' I said. 'Sure they could have been accidental, but let's imagine they were lit deliberately. As it was, they burned through a valley parallel to this one. The smoke spilled over in this direction and clung to the hills but the fire wasn't likely to cut back on itself. What if it had been set on the road side of the location? It would have destroyed the set – the walls, the palace, every damn thing. End of production. The producers would have pulled the plug. The arsonist could have scuttled the movie right there. But this way we just lost two days of shooting.'

'And that explains why OB will be returning this afternoon?' Lizzie said sarcastically.

'Oh, do shut up,' Bunny snapped. The gofer gave her a killing look.

I continued.

'It was the same with the cameras. I don't have any idea how you'd put a spanner in the works there but it was just enough to lose another day-and-a-half of production, not to shut it down. They want this movie to hang on here in Fang for as long as possible. Lizzie, do you know off hand what the overrun period is? How many days over the schedule can the budget absorb?'

'It's usually no more than a week before they'd cut their losses and see what they can do in a studio back in the states,' she said.

'Okay, then, by whatever means they'll get those seven extra days.'

'But, what for?' Kuro asked.

'The oldest crime in the world, Kuro san.'

Khin raised her eyebrows and smiled.

'No, Khin, even older than that. It even got a mention in the Ten Commandments. Good old-fashioned stealing – theft – grand larceny.'

'Who's stealing from whom?' Bunny asked.

'The Fang police are stealing from those extras out there.'

'That is a considerable amount of effort for a few dorrars a day,' Kuro decided.

'That's what I thought, till I got out the calculator,' I said. 'Lizzie, how much is the movie paying extras?'

'Well ...'

'I need the actual figure, not what the unions tell you to pay.'

'Thirty bucks a day plus meals.'

'Hmm, lucky they didn't get around to joining actor's equity. But anyway, thirty dollars is a good day's work for someone whose annual income's no more than three hundred. Do you hand it to the extras directly?'

'We don't walk around with suitcases full of cash, if that's what you mean. We make daily bank deposits into the Northern Thai Castings account.'

'Alias the Fang police force.'

'What? You're saying they aren't passing the money on to the extras?'

'The extras are getting a hundred and twenty *baht* a day from Northern Castings. That's if he ever turns up with the cash. That's about three dollars fifty. That means twenty-six dollars fifty goes into the pocket of the police. And that's why they recruited people who couldn't speak Thai or English and why they told them not to talk to anyone apart from their foreman. Because, now we see how the bucks start mounting up. Two thousand times twenty-six fifty is ... Khin?'

'Fifty-three thousand dollars.'

'Thanks.'

'You're welcome.'

'Originally, they were hired for nine days – contribution to the police retirement fund ...'

'Four hundred and seventy-seven thousand dollars,' said Khin without pausing.

'And, let's assume they get their full seven days of overtime ...'

'A grand total of eight hundred and forty-eight thousand dollars,' said Khin.

'Add to that the police helicopters and limos and drivers, and their cut from the elephants and etceteras, and we're well on the happy side of a million bucks.'

Everybody but Khin said, 'Shit'.

I continued. 'Now, I know a million is but a peanut to a forty million dollar movie production but it's a hell of an incentive to a Thai police major on an annual salary of under ten-thousand dollars. So, you see? They don't want OB dead. I imagine they hired some local thugs to kidnap him and ask for a ransom. The police will bravely raid the kidnappers' lair and overcome them. Major Ketthai shows up here on his white horse with OB holding on behind him. The studio's extremely grateful and show's its gratitude – perhaps pays for a new bridge or an airport. The director's shaken but not damaged. A day of shooting is lost but the show goes on.'

I turned to Bunny. 'I imagine around next Tuesday you and Jensen would have contracted food-poisoning or some other debilitating illness for a day just to keep things slowed down.'

'Wow!' Bunny smiled. 'You're Sherlock Holmes.'

'Elementary,' said Khin. 'All but for the fact that the actual Mrs. Holmes would now take her findings to Scotland Yard and leave the arrests up to the constabulary. We, on the other hand are in a country run by an illegal military junta and our complaint is against the Royal Thai Police force. I'm at a loss as to with whom you are intending to share this astounding revelation.'

There passed a few seconds of silence.

'I know,' said Sissy.

'Know what?' I asked.

'I know who to tell. I know a guy. I went out with him. We kept in touch. He works for the Counter Corruption Commission in Bangkok.'

'That's the military,' I said.

'Not really,' he replied. 'I mean, yeah, they have military connections but officially they're independent. They have investigators and undercover people. And, don't worry. There isn't a lot of love lost between the army and the police. If we put together the evidence I reckon he can help us out.'

'In a hurry?' Bunny asked.

'He has people based in Chiang Mai.'

'Then go get him, boy,' I said.

'Can I get a fast ride into Tha Ton?' Sissy asked Lizzie.

'You just want to phone?'

'Yeah.'

'We've got satellite in the command tent.'

Chapter 29

"But we only have fourteen hours to save the Earth!"
Flash Gordon (1980)

It was evening. The national and international press had been tipped off about the disappearance of OB and they'd swarmed like rain ants to the movie sight. They'd spilled out of the roped-off observer area and were making a nuisance of themselves interviewing the crew and actors. The police had shepherded all the Wa extras to a field a kilometer away.

Despite the fact that he didn't have a clue what was going on around him, Dan Jensen had called an impromptu press conference. With Tony in his arms he maintained his rugged frontiersman demeanour whilst inadvertently releasing one small photogenic tear that lingered on his cheek. He described the father/son relationship he'd established with the director and had been praying to both God and the Lord Buddha for his safe return. With nothing to do but wait, we availed ourselves of the food and beverages in the canteen trailer until we heard a commotion outside. People were running, someone shouting, 'He's back'.

On the set we encountered a movie scene within a movie scene. It was reality cinema – staged yet spontaneous. A cameraman on the scaffold filmed the proceedings without direction. Major Ketthai had arrived at the set. From our vantage point on a small hill we could see the entrance to the site and the valley. A short convoy of cars had come to a halt just below us. The lead vehicle was the gold SUV in front of which stood the major answering questions from the Thai press. OB was standing beside him looking tired and a little bemused.

The sounds of the interview microphone reverberated in the valley. Ketthai held up the rope that had tethered the director and the knife with which the major had cut him loose. There had been a tragic gun fight which left the kidnappers dead. Their bodies wrapped in large blue sheets of plastic were in the back of a pickup truck behind the SUV. On a second pickup a heavily armed squad of commando-like police officers sat stiffly. They were dressed in black and shouldered assault weapons. Their cheeks had been darkened with charcoal rectangles that I realized served no purpose other than looking impressive in photographs.

OB gazed around him and noticed us on the ridge. He waved slowly and we raised our thumbs. The gesture didn't necessarily suggest that everything had come to a happy conclusion. I had no idea what to expect next. After his phone call, Sissy had gone off to meet his friend's contacts in Tha Ton and nobody had heard from him since. It was possible the CCC wouldn't be at all interested in a small corrupt police force in the north. They were busy sorting through charges against the entire cabinet of the deposed prime-minister. They had a year to bring them to justice and reclaim any siphoned-off finances before the country reverted to its usual warped democracy.

It wasn't unthinkable that Major Ketthai might become a world media celebrity the next day – a real life hero for the new millennium. It was likely he'd receive a commendation from the police ministry and be promoted to an influential position. Such things happened in Thailand. If corruption was handled neatly enough the common people would respect you for getting away with it.

The crew, staff and Thai extras had gathered around the convoy. Some were photographing the wrapped bodies with their mobile phones, others were posing with the somber swat team. I knew the Wa had been moved away yet I could see there were some bold characters stripped to the waist working their way toward the convoy. They were approaching from different directions like insects that had the scent of a dropped sugar lozenge. They filtered through the onlookers and seemed intent on getting as close to the trucks as they could.

It was a scene that could only have been noticed from an elevated angle. The police officers in the truck and the press gathered around OB would have spotted nothing unusual. Some of the newcomers were shaking hands with the commandos and slapping them on the back.

Then there must have come an order that I could neither see nor hear and the bare-chested extras, to a man, reached behind their backs and produced pistols from the bands of their shorts. With just one brief scuffle the police in the truck were overwhelmed. Two men stood either side of Major Ketthai and his adjutant with guns pointed into their sides. They removed the weapons from the policemen's holsters. Two uniformed army officers arrived and held up their hands to the frantic press gallery. Cameras clicked and whirred and questions were yelled. One of the soldiers began to address them in Thai. The foreign press was even more frustrated.

'What's he saying?' Bunny asked.

'He's telling them the story,' I said.

'Beginning?'

I listened.

'Right at the start,' I said. 'The threat to Star Castings in Bangkok and the transfer of the contract to Northern Thai.'

'They knew about that?'

'So it seems. It's pretty detailed. I guess ...'

'What?'

From the scrum of onlookers below someone had called Sissy forward. He was wearing denim overalls and had darkened his five-o-clock shadow to appear in front of the cameras. He stood beside OB and began a translation for the foreign correspondents. Nobody wanted to miss a word.

'I guess Sissy passed the message on to his friend,' I said to the group gathered around me. 'But I get the idea the army boys have been monitoring this already. You don't set up a sting operation this fast.'

'You should be down there too,' said Bunny.

'That's not going to happen.'

'Why not?'

'I'm shy.'

Four army vehicles rolled up the dirt path from the road and the disarmed police were loaded aboard. Major Ketthai, shouting his innocence and calling for the press not to believe the word of an illegal military junta, was hurried into a jeep and driven away. Only Sissy, OB and the two military officers remained in front of the gallery. After ten minutes, the tale was almost told.

'The military took over the police headquarters in Fang half an hour ago and removed all the files and computers,' Sissy was saying. 'The suspects will be held by the army until the central police command in Bangkok has time to go through all the evidence.'

'He's good, isn't he,' said Bunny.

'A natural.'

Chapter 30

"It's been a long time since I smelled beautiful."
The Chronicles of Riddick (2004)

The balcony party that night was seriously silly. We'd somehow crushed the entire crew, the international and Thai actors and two dozen legitimate journalists into the accountant's house. Even Dan Jensen had somehow found his way to the celebrations. There was just the one official camerawoman and she seemed to be caught up in the gravity of the stars. The gate security was on double shift. The drinks cabinet was emptied very early in the piece but OB had bought out the entire stock of the *Mini Mart and Drink*, Tha Ton's own general store. Even that was in danger of early depletion and one of the drivers had been sent into Fang to hunt for more.

'So, OB tells me you and your brothers are leaving the picture.' Bunny had joined me on the two-person swing seat in the side garden.

'Yeah. We've done enough dying for one year.'

We listened to a green-headed gecko yelling its chant above the din of the CD speakers. Sissy had pointed out once that if you listened carefully it sounded like it was saying 'Take care, take care,' but I'd never been able to hear that. Bunny told me I should be inside having a good time but I wasn't in a mingling mood. I spent most of the following two hours on that swing seat and let the party come to me. I felt like Larry King. Everyone came to talk. One celebrity stood up and another took his or her place. I had my pick of second string actors that night but all I could think of was how close we'd come to losing our lives. Khin wasn't amongst the glitterati of course. She'd taken the night bus back to Chiang Mai. She had more important things on her mind than murder and corruption. Before she left, an arrangement had been made for the Wa to stay on and see out the contract at the official rate of thirty-dollars a day. It transpired that the Wa Army would be helping themselves to half of the hundred and twenty *baht* wages as 'commission'. If the extras could keep their mouths shut they'd have a healthy nest egg left at the end of it. For some it meant a chance to pay off debts and start a new life.

To my disappointment, Khin hadn't forgotten the deal we'd made. Her parting comment had been, 'I'll make the Wieng Kum Kam house as comfortable as possible for your arrival. You should all bring shovels. It shouldn't take us more than a week to find our pot of gold.'

OB had come to join me on the swing seat.

'We're going to miss you guys,' he said. 'Not on the set so much, but you'll be notable absentees from our philosophy nights on the balcony.'

'What do you mean, not on the set?' I said. 'You don't think I could make it in Hollywood?'

'No.'

'Ah, I hate honesty.'

'You wouldn't want the Hollywood life. It affects people in all the worst ways. You've got all the heaven you need right here.'

'You seem to have gotten through it in one piece.'

'This is me at the end of the tunnel,' he said. 'I went through a number of dark identities before I arrived at this one.'

'Well, I like it. Hang on to it.'

'Thanks Jimm.'

Sissy made a few brief stopovers at the swing seat. He brought me refills for my Chilean red.

'Hey, brother,' I said.

'Any news about …'

The music stopped when someone changed the stack of CDs.

'… the body we dumped in the river?' he asked too loudly.

Heads turned but we were only briefly embarrassed. We laughed as if it was a punch line and the people standing around in the garden went back to their small talk. The music started. Mary J Blige.

'Shout it a little bit louder why don't you?' I said.

'Sorry.'

'They got two descriptions from your lady at Star Castings. The guy in our living room was probably the private eye she hired to look for her girlfriend. But that body hasn't shown up yet so we can't be sure.'

'And the girlfriend?'

'Some workers at a pomelo plantation told the military they'd seen a woman's body in a pond. It was pretty rotten but it might have been the partner. Looks like she was tortured before they shot her.'

'Shit. It's a messed up world, Jimm.'

'It sure is.'

'Any theories about why Director Boon got himself shot?' Sissy asked.

'I'm guessing he found out the extras were getting ripped off and didn't want any part of it,' I said. 'The cops pulled the same intimidation trick that had worked on the CEO in Bangkok. But he didn't have family to threaten and they knew his reputation so I'd bet they were afraid he'd go to the authorities. The meeting was the deadline. If he didn't show up with the money they had no choice but to execute him.'

'Poor guy,' said Arny. 'This is a tough life for honest people.'

'Yeah.'

'Which reminds me. Did Khin forget?'

'Sadly, not.'

'So we've still got to go down there and dig?'

'I'm sorry. I did kind of promise her.'

'It's okay. She deserves it.'

To my surprise, even Dan Jensen came over to pay his respects on the swing seat.

'Wow, you know everybody,' he said. 'Who are you?'

'I'm you.'

'Yeah? Zen.'

'Where's your dog?'

'He goes to bed at seven.'

'Beauty sleep?'

'Something like.'

'Dan?'

'Yeah, man?'

'Are you into boys?'

'What? A guy has a miniature dog so he has to be a faggot?' He'd lowered his voice and pushed the frontiersman out in front of him. 'Jees!'

'Sorry.'

Jensen looked at me. I gave him my prettiest smile.

'Why you asking, anyway?' he asked.

'Well, you're a cute guy. I was just … oh, nothing.'

'Are you hitting on me?'

'Well, it's just you're the only guy here who hasn't propositioned me yet so I guess you haven't heard about my … unique gift.'

Jensen seemed to blush and looked away. That really would have been a coup – bedded by the male lead of a big Hollywood movie. He turned back to me and French kissed me. He tasted of Lysterene. It was an oddly pleasant moment but he ruined it.

'I could give you a go,' he said. 'Can't say I've had a Thai chick before. But you do know I could have my pick of anyone?'

So when he came back later to tell me he'd missed his helicopter and asked me where my room was I gave him directions to OB's suite. I told him he could bed down early and wait for a surprise. That tickled me, the thought of him not getting lucky for once in his life.

Chapter 31

"Constantly talking isn't necessarily communicating."
Eternal Sunshine of the Spotless Mind (2004)

'Khin, put those charts away and come have a drink why don't you?'

My suggestion was ignored. She and Sissy and Arny sat in front of the building with their feet on a saggy, half-rolled chicken-wire fence that was unlikely to deter even the most undetermined chicken. As there'd been no chairs to move out into the concrete front yard Sissy had removed the seats from his jeep and lined them up behind the fence. It was a poor substitute for the house on Doi Suthep.

'I feel like a redneck,' I said.

Our view was of the bungalow directly opposite and the old lady's grey underwear hanging from a line.

'Khin!'

'Yes, I'm coming.'

After two days at home recovering from the excitement we'd arrived in Wieng Kum Kam that morning. We'd spent most of the day pacing and sinking probes and scratching at the earth with spoons. I was surprised nobody had come to ask what we were doing. There was no guard or watchman as such. The head of the village was technically in charge of the site only because the ruins were in his suburb. But he didn't seem particularly interested in its historic significance. He liked the fact that tourists came and injected modest sums into the local businesses. But, like me, he felt little love for the piles of bricks all around.

At present there was no team from the Fine Arts Department working at Wieng Kum Kam. They came and they went with the budget. Right now, with the military occupation, a number of project funds had been frozen. Khin had flashed her CMU letter at the headman who read as far as 'university' and 'Burmese expert', and asked her if she needed a place to rent and a 'companion'. She assumed this meant a lady housekeeper to avert the normal dangers encountered by single women rather than a lover. Khin had accepted the room but declined the chaperone. It had been a bad decision all round.

But it wasn't just the depressing house, the wasted effort and the view of the neighbour's underwear that caused the atmosphere of gloom that evening. During the afternoon Sissy had received a call from his friend at the CCC. It appeared that two of the senior officers at the Fang station had been identified both on the film at the Dhara Dehvi and as the heavies who visited Tip at Star Castings. But there had been no concrete evidence to implicate Major Ketthai and none of his men was prepared to give evidence against him. They all seemed to believe that, come the November elections, it would be business as usual in the country and their cases would be dismissed.

The military junta had no legal right to hold Major Ketthai and under pressure from the interim crime suppression division commissioner he had been released. A considerable bail sum had been ordered and summarily posted. Sissy's friend had strongly recommended that we lay low for a while. The major had been overheard talking about the interfering bastards from Chiang Mai. He'd given the impression he wasn't familiar with the concept of gentlemanly defeat. To our knowledge there had been four deaths to date, and two more wouldn't add to or subtract from the major's account in Hell. It wasn't unthinkable that the Fang policeman might seek revenge.

We had reached the end of our seething and were currently in a funk that only a drink and a smoke could lift. Khin had to duck as she came out through the doorway and plonked herself down into the passenger seat. I handed her a glass of neat Saeng Som rum. Ice might have made it more palatable but there was no refrigerator and the local shop closed at six.

'I remain baffled,' Khin admitted. She drank from the glass with a lack of expression. No food nor drink had ever inspired Khin to make a comment about it. She was either empty or full like a VW gas tank. On approaching empty she refuelled. She could eat anything at any time – the spiciest Thai dishes or the most flyblown roadside lunches.

'I fear I may have erred in some way,' she said.

We weren't surprised in the least. We expected no better from our eccentric friend. I'd listened to her foolproof plan and failed to follow her. But it was good to have our minds off Major Ketthai.

'It clearly stated,' Khin blustered on, 'that Mangrai had supported a temple at the furthest point from the river. The two most distant temples within the city walls were Phan Lao and Hua Nong. None of the other buildings we see here today had been built in Mangrai's time. I have identified and located these two temples and we have covered every inch of ground within the eastern moat and been unable to find any remains of the other temple mentioned in the transcripts – the temple they refer to as Pa Tan, which may be translated as the palm toddy temple.'

'Maybe they were suffering from overcrowding and they had to build it outside the city,' I suggested. I liked to show Khin I had some interest in her research even though I did not.

'Yes, Jimm,' she said. 'As I have explained many times, in the thirteenth century, one of the main points of building a walled city was to safeguard one's Buddha images and valuables. It was extremely unlikely Mangrai would have favoured a temple that didn't fall within the security of the city.'

'But not impossible.'

'Unlikely in the extreme.'

We were tired of doing the 'what-ifs'. I looked at my watch to see how many minutes remained of our three-day commitment.

'Khin, relax,' said Arny. 'You'll see things a lot clearer in the morning.'

'Perhaps you're right,' Khin conceded and finished her drink. She was already starting to slur.

We sat back in our seats and contemplated the ridiculousness of our predicament. The neighbours opposite gazed out of their window from time to time and made fun of the rednecks in the bomb shelter. There came the sound of a car engine meandering through the labyrinth of tiny lanes. Initially it gave us hope that there would be something to look at other than the uninspiring neighbourhood. But then the thought of a passing car – Major Ketthai and a drive-by shooting - occurred to each of us. Nobody wanted to own up to the fact that we were afraid of the major so we sat in silence as the vehicle got closer. How could he know where we were anyway?

This was a small quiet community with little space to park a car and no cause to go gallivanting around at night. We heard the car stop a block away, the distant sound of voices, of laughter, the slam of a car door, first gear, second. Headlights on full beam rounded the corner at the end of Khin's narrow street. My brothers and I tensed and prepared to run amok. The lights blinded us but they were low to the ground, not the headlights of an SUV. The vehicle crawled up to a front gate along the street and the driver killed the lights. Immediately we were able to make out the logo of an old taxi. The driver was a neighbour. We quenched our dry throats in unison.

Time passed as slowly as an ice floe. The mosquito coil emitted a pall of smoke so white and thick that the mosquitoes held back and waited for it to pass before settling on fresh meat.

'Damn it,' Arny screamed at one more mosquito. 'How come I'm the only one that gets bitten?'

''Cause you're tasty,' I told him. 'The rest of us are just old meat and bone.'

I looked sideways at Khin and studied the downturn of her mouth.

'Why so glum, Khin?'

'She's still sulking 'cause she's lost a temple,' said Sissy.

'It's true,' said Khin. 'I am a little down in the dumps. I had been very much hoping we would be able to begin excavation work tomorrow. The signs had been favourable.'

'You really think they'd just let us walk in and dig up their ruins?' I asked.

'You have seen the official map,' she said. 'They believe that they have discovered all there is to discover. The temple we are seeking does not officially exist. We would in fact be doing them a favour.'

'Except we can't find it either,' Sissy reminded him.

'Do you think it could be under one of these houses?' Arny asked.

'That regrettably, is the only conclusion I have been able to reach. Short of knocking them all down and digging through the rubble, I'm afraid that would be the end of our search.'

'I reckon you've been holding the map upside down, Khin,' I said.

'There, the rational sound of reason,' said Khin. 'Such wisdom inspires me to …'

She put down her glass and staggered to her feet.

'… go to the toilet.'

They watched her weave her way into the house.

'Come on guys,' Arny said. 'She needs help, not ridicule.'

'Yeah, counselling,' I suggested.

'A psychiatrist even,' added Sissy.

'She's your friend,' said Arny.

'Yeah, I know,' I said. 'This is how we show our love. We keep her excitement levels down so she doesn't get too disappointed.'

'You've been through this before?'

'A dozen or so times.'

'Poor woman,' said Arny. 'Hey, I couldn't help noticing there isn't any bedding, inside.'

'Right,' I agreed. 'It's like camping.'

'I'm all into that,' he said, 'but the floor's like concrete.'

'It is concrete. I thought you were here for the adventure,' Sissy smiled.

'I am. I am, but ...'

'Sissy,' I said, 'don't give the boy a hard time. We aren't going to sleep here, my prince. It's only twenty minutes drive home. We'll come back tomorrow morning.'

'And Khin?'

'There's a wafer thin mattress out the back,' I told him. 'She's Burmese. This is luxury. And I'd say now's as good a time as any to leave her to her thoughts.'

While Sissy and Arny put the seats back in the jeep, I went through to the outside facility to tell Khin we were off. The garden latrine was a five feet high bamboo affair with no roof. Khin's head was not visible above the fence line so I had to assume she'd thrown herself into the pit.

'Hey, Khin,' I shouted. 'Don't get up, girl ... Khin?'

There was no answer. Against my better judgment, I leaned over the bamboo and glanced inside. It wasn't a pretty sight but there was no sign of the Burmese. The back yard was bordered by a high brick wall on two sides which formed the perimeter of yet another temple. On the third side was another chicken-wire fence. It separated the yard from one of the few remaining rice paddies in Wieng Kum Kam. At some stage, the fence had been trampled to the ground. The paddy field was dry and it was too dark to see beyond it.

'Khin?'

I scratched my head and walked back through the house, looking to either side but not really expecting to find her wedged in a corner. My brothers were working on the rear seat.

'What time's the general want us back?' Sissy asked.

'She's not there,' I said.

'What do you mean?'

'I mean she's vanished.'

'She went to the toilet,' said Arny.

'I know she did, but she's not there now.'

'Did you check?' he asked.

'Did I check what?'

'The pit in there's pretty deep.'

'Arny, it's an eighteen inch hole. Khin's skinny enough but it'd take a pile driver …'

'She's clumsy, Jimm.'

'Arny, she didn't fall down the latrine.'

'Well, she didn't come through this way,' he said. 'Let's have a look.'

We went out to the back yard and surveyed the scene. We agreed the walls were too high to climb which only left the fence and the rice field beyond.

'Anyone recall the fence being beaten down when we first got here?' Sissy asked.

Nobody did.

'Did she have a flashlight?' asked Arny.

I went inside and found Khin's flashlight in her pack. Beyond the light from the house, there was no way to see your way through the field and the ruins beyond without one. The masked March moon didn't shed any light.

'So, either Khin has gone running off into the pitch darkness without a light …,' I began, then realized the second alternative wasn't as far fetched as I might have intended.'

'Or?' Arny urged.

'Or she's been kidnapped,' said Sissy.

We were at a loss as to what to do next. If she were a five-year-old or a granny with Alzheimer's we'd have rushed off into the surrounding neighbourhood banging on doors, calling out in desperation, organizing a search. But she was Khin and she'd survived the Burmese junta and the history department at CMU.

We closed her front door and rode leisurely around all the sites in the order that Khin had first introduced them. We drove on high beam on the off chance we might catch her sparkly-eyed and frozen in the middle of the trail, but no luck. We returned to the earthen rampart where we'd stood for the better part of the day prodding and spooning. No Khin. We returned to the house – still dark and Khinless.

It was midnight. We sat in the car and decided to give up till morning. If anyone had wanted her dead they would have done her in right there in the garden rather than drag her over a field. If she'd been kidnapped we could expect a ransom note, although Sissy suggested anyone foolish enough to kidnap Khin would be illiterate. The mystery of Khin's disappearance had to be put on pause till the sun came up. By the time we reached the family shop we'd all settled into a comfortable denial.

Chapter 32

"Water can carve its way even through stone ... and when trapped, water makes a new path."
Memoires of a Geisha (2005)

It was seven or thereabouts when we arrived back at Khin's. None of us had slept. Going home had been a mistake. We pulled up in front of the house and the first thing we noticed was the open front door. We went inside and found Khin sitting cross-legged on the concrete floor of the kitchen area eating rice porridge from the plastic bags it was sold in. She looked as if she'd cut herself shaving thirty or forty times. I walked over to her and pinched her earlobe hard enough to elicit an 'Ow!'

'Khin, you scrawny coat hanger,' I raised my voice. 'Don't you give a shit what you put your friends through?'

She blushed a little and smiled but didn't offer up an apology. We sat on the floor in a circle.

'Go ahead, Khin,' I said. 'What happened?'

Khin wiped her mouth before answering.

'Very well,' she said. 'I was in the toilet doing...what one does when one is in the toilet. I completed my mission and I scooped the receptacle into the water bucket behind me.'

I interrupted her.

'This isn't going to be a play by play of you wiping your ass?'

She ignored the question.

'At the back of my mind,' she continued, 'was your facetious parting comment that I may have been looking at the map upside down.'

'Oh, man, you weren't?' said Arny.

'I was sloshing the water and thinking and sloshing and thinking,' she said. 'And I looked into the hole and I saw ...'

'Khin!'

'... I saw the layers of earth and silt. This was the silt that has encased many of the edifices in Wieng Kum Kam. In a number of situations it was what protected them from natural erosion and preserved them. The silt came from the river. So, as I sloshed, I began to ask myself why the city was so given to flooding. The river passes to the southwest of the town and the land there is notably lower. I wondered why Mangrai would build a city on land that was known to flood each year.'

'And?' Arny asked.

'And he didn't,' she replied. 'According to the chronicles, he diverted the flow of the Ping river to fill the moat around the city. It was this diversion that caused the flooding and he had no way of readjusting its course.'

'Your grandpa Mangrai screwed up the ecology,' I grinned at Sissy.

'So, what's this got to do with the price of prawns?' Sissy asked.

Khin went on.

'Sissy, water flows downhill. As the Ping passes to the southwest of Wieng Kum Kam, it can only mean one thing.'

'What?'

'The river's changed its course,' she said with a smile.

'I hope someone's following this,' I said, shaking my head.

Khin beamed, 'In the thirteenth century the river did not pass the city to the southwest. It originally traversed the northeast corner. When it was diverted into the moat it found its own level.'

'So?'

'So we have been searching for an unknown temple that was described as being farthest from the river. In fact, what was farthest from the river to Mangrai, is nearest to the river in modern times. We have been looking in the wrong place.'

I rolled my eyes, not for the first time, 'You surprise me.'

'What now?' Arny asked.

'We change flanks,' she said. 'We regroup and recommence our search on the opposite side of the old city. I assure you all, the adventure has just begun.'

Arny clapped his hands and whooped.

'This is so exciting,' he said.

'I'm all aquiver,' hummed Sissy.

'Me too,' I yawned.

Khin redrew the map. She pencilled in the Ping river passing the city to the northeast. It made a lot more sense. They'd built Wieng Kum Kam near the river and dug a trench to feed the moat. Rivers don't take too kindly to coercion and throughout history there were common accounts of the ancient city being flooded.

'If this theory holds water, if you'll excuse my pun,' Khin told us, 'the original river passed here.'

She pointed to the grey line on her map.

'The furthest point from it within the original city confines would be around here.'

She marked the potential site with a large circle and at least half of that circle fell upon the present Ping River.

'The department of Fine Arts has no thirteenth century temples listed in this area. Given their thorough investigation of the site I was perplexed that they had found nothing at all. But then again, temples and stupas were added to the site right up until the beginning of the seventeenth century when Wieng Kum Kam vanished from historical sight. It was logical that they would avoid building too close to the temperamental Ping. We need to turn a blind eye to any later constructions and visualize the city as it looked at the turn of the fourteenth century. King Mangrai approaching Nirvana decides to build a *chedi* and bury the dynasty's treasure. I can almost sense it. Feel it.'

Sissy ran his fingers through his hair samurai fashion and hissed.

'So, Khin. All this came to you while you were taking a dump?'

'In the aftermath.'

'And it inspired you to abandon your guests without a word, tear down your garden fence, and go groping your way through the dark to the river.'

'Oh, no. All I had to do was climb the wall. We are comparatively close to the river. I used the ladder to go over the wall to the compound.'

'We didn't see a ladder,' I said.

'Of course not. I had to use the same ladder to climb down the other side of the wall. When I realized what had happened yesterday evening, I was so excited I went immediately to the riverbank to survey possibilities. Sadly it was too dark to do a thorough search. I got a little scratched by the bushes. But I have a very strong intuition about this. I believe I know why the department of Fine Arts found nothing in their search.'

'Yeah, okay, Khin,' I said. 'So what's our chore for the day?'

'Goodness me, Jimm,' she said. 'Please display some enthusiasm. We are on the cusp.'

I didn't know what a cusp was and it didn't cheer my mood at all that we might be on one. I didn't even have the enthusiasm to ask.

'Professor Khin,' Sissy said. He stood, saluted and clicked his heels together. 'Your wish is our command. We serve at your pleasure. Direct us.'

I rose languidly to my feet and joined the line up. Only two more days. Only two more days.

Chapter 33

"To the last, I will grapple with thee ... from Hell's heart, I stab at thee! For hate's sake, I spit my last breath at thee!"
Star Trek: The Wrath of Khan (1982)

Khin posited that the current course of the river might have been directed by an irrigation ditch or trench running at the back of the old city. Fortifications were famous for moats and deep gullies filled with frightful wooden stakes. Such a trench would act as a natural conduit for flood water and eventually define a new course for the river. If the Pa Tan Temple had been built flush with the rear fortifications it could well have been overwhelmed by the new river at the same time as the missing rear wall.

The day's objective was to walk the length of the river to the west of Wieng Kum Kam and take a note of the topography. Any mounds in unexpected places or sudden dips, or islands mid river had to be noted. The way Khin told it, the mission was an enjoyable stroll on a river bank. But time and neglect had left the riverside overgrown and wild. Even getting close to the bank was a safari. There was one vague trail that led to a fenced-off area with a metal gate.

'What do they want to keep us out of?' Arny asked.

'I think it's the other way round,' Khin said, squeezing through a gap at the side of the gate. 'My local shop owner tells me there were people arriving in boats in the dead of night and sailing away with bricks for their patios and garden walls. I believe a lot went missing before the department invested in this gate.'

'Well, it really is a deterrent,' I agreed and hopped over the top of it. Sissy threw over the equipment bags and the packed lunch then he and Arny joined us on the other side. It was starting to feel like an adventure at last. We arrived at the water's edge on a small sandy landing, and stared up and down stream. The unruly vegetation lurched out into the water in either direction and thick reeds clogged the shoreline.

'You expect us to fight through all that?' I asked. 'I mean, shit, Khin.'

'I did manage to get a fair way into the jungle last night,' she boasted.

'Which explains the whip marks,' I said. 'We'd need native scouts and machetes to get through this.'

'I can think of a faster and a much more fun way to do this,' said Arny as he slowly unbuckled his belt and lowered his jeans.

'What the hell are you doing?' I asked.

'It's okay. I'm wearing undies.'

He kicked off his shoes and stepped out of his jeans. It was true. He was wearing underwear but not the type Sister Denise at Saint Martin's would have let pass the inspection. He pulled his T-shirt over his head and posed briefly for the audience.

'Goodness,' said Khin. 'You should be in movies.'

Arny laughed and walked into the water.

The Ping was flowing slowly and was a lot cleaner in March than in the rainy season when all the mud ran off the denuded mountains and turned it into cocoa.

'It's great,' he shouted and launched off into an elegant front crawl.

'I guess that's the answer,' said Sissy, wrestling himself out of his clothes. Externally, he was kitted out bisexually but wore a pretty yellow bra and panties beneath. He went crashing down the bank and headfirst into the Ping.

'Yes, well … it would undoubtedly save us some time,' Khin conceded. 'It's just that …'

'What is it Khin?'

'I have inadvertently left home without my underwear on. I washed it all this morning when I returned from my adventure and they are still damp on the line.'

So Khin dived in wearing her staypress rayon slacks and long-sleeved salmon blouse. I followed in shorts and T-shirt. We would have won a best dressed swimmers in the Ping competition. After a short playful swim to get ourselves in the mood we began to wade close to the bank. Sissy and I went upstream, Arny and Khin, down. She'd calculated that we'd only need to go four-hundred meters in either direction. But even that is a considerable distance when you're up to your shins in mud. We hadn't gone much more than fifty meters before we heard Khin's excited falsetto 'yoohoo' from around the bend.

'This way,' she called. 'Over here.'

We let the current carry us down to where Khin and Arny stood in the water staring at what could only be described as a small bump the size of a Chinese burial mound. It was criss-crossed with dead and dying vines and gnarled with weeds.

'What's that, Khin?' I asked.

'Well, it could be a very large rock,' she replied, 'although we aren't anywhere close to any outcrops at all. Or it could be a structure of some kind covered in silt and earth …'

'Or, it could be a little hill,' I added.

Khin turned to me.

'Jimm, over time, a river has a habit of removing hills from its path and levelling the land. If it were just an earthen hill this close to the river I doubt it would still be in existence.'

'So, what do we do?' Arny asked.

'We retrieve our packs, break out our digging equipment and dig,' she said.

Ten minutes later we were back at the mound pulling away the vegetation and gently digging down through the soil. It was just as well none of us was squeamish because we disturbed a menagerie of crawlers and scurriers. Sissy, who had been entrusted with a small garden trowel, was the first to hit pay dirt. We all heard the dull thud and looked up.

'That sounded like gold to me,' said Arny.

'Yes, I'm afraid it isn't going to be quite as simple as that,' Khin warned him.

We dug around the mystery object and, to nobody's surprise, it turned out to be a brick. Khin produced a notebook from her pack and began to draw a diagram of the mound and the exact position of the brick in relation to it.

'Khin, it's a brick,' I pointed out, 'and you can be pretty sure there'll be more where that came from.'

Khin lifted her chin.

'And I shall document each one,' she said. 'Let us not forget that this brick could have been forged seven hundred years ago. The last person to touch it was probably a Mangrai dynasty tradesman. We have to uncover this structure as carefully as we can to preserve its identity.'

We worked slowly down through the mound for the entire morning. Arny went off to get cold drinks to wash down our lunch and after a brief rest we began to work into the afternoon. We were shaded by a sprawling jujube tree but by mid-afternoon the breezes had died and the temperature had hit thirty-four degrees. Our play times in the water grew longer and our skins redder. The enthusiasm of all but Khin began to wane when it grew clear that the bricks in the mound yielded no pattern whatsoever. What we had discovered was not a structure but a brick heap.

Still, Khin was excited.

'They are clearly very very early bricks,' she told her dispirited co-workers.

'From the composition and shape I'd have to say they're certainly pre-fifteenth century.'

'So, what are they doing here?' I asked.

'That is a very good question.'

'No shortage of questions, that's for sure,' I mumbled.

Arny, as usual, was more positive.

'Are you certain it isn't the ruins of a temple that fell down?'

'It is clear that we have come to the bottom of the pile,' Khin told him, 'and there is no evidence of a foundation. Any stupa or edifice would have certainly collapsed onto its own base.'

'Then it's just a pile of bricks they were going to use to build something,' Sissy suggested, 'but the union rep didn't like the management's conditions and called his guys out.'

Khin sidestepped the levity.

'But look here, Sissy,' she said, holding up a brick from the heap. 'You can clearly see the crude mortared edging. These were once part of some edifice.'

We watched her mind tick over.

'But what could have brought them here to this heap? Why weren't they reused in subsequent constructions? Never mind. Let's push on. I suggest we continue our survey of the riverbank and see if there are any other topographical anomalies.'

'And I suggest we go home, have a shower and a cold beer or two,' I said.

'And I second that,' said Sissy.

'But comrades, the day is still young.'

'And we're getting older by the minute,' I said. 'We've been at it since eight this morning. Give us a break, woman.'

'You're right,' Khin said, trying to disguise the hurt on her face. 'I apologize. Please, you have been extremely helpful, all of you. I thank you. But if you don't mind I shall continue here whilst there is still daylight. There is much to be done.'

'You sure?' Sissy asked.

'Yes,' she said. 'I feel certain I shall have some good news for you when we reunite tomorrow.'

'One more day,' I said as we walked away. 'One more day.'

We felt bad leaving Khin alone with her bricks but we'd really had enough dirt for one day. We waded back upstream with our packs on our heads like bearers in the Amazon. We climbed over the gate and walked back toward Khin's house where the jeep was parked. We sat briefly atop the wall like birds and swung the ladder to the yard side. When Arny and I were down, Sissy swung it back for Khin's return then lowered himself onto Arny's shoulders.

There was nothing to delay us at the house. Not even the garden latrine reached out to us for a visit. We could hold any business we had till we got home. We entered through the rear door and I noticed how strangely dark it was inside. The curtains were drawn, the front door closed with a margin of light around its frame barely showing us the way. Something was odd. Then we heard the voice. The words, spoken in unpolished northern Thai, seemed to emerge naturally from the gloom.

'What kept you so long?'

Arny squealed in surprise and Sissy turned to the back door only to be blocked by the muzzle of an automatic rifle pointed at his head. Now there was movement in the house and it was apparent there were figures lurking around the walls in the shadows. Someone pulled one of the curtains back a crack. Three men in jeans and white T-shirts were spaced around the room armed and pointing their weapons at us. Major Ketthai sat on Khin's rolled-up mattress against the far wall.

'Sit down,' he ordered. 'All of you.'

'No chairs, pal,' said Sissy.

The man behind him jabbed his gun between my brother's shoulder blades with a thump and sent him crashing forward onto his knees. Arny took hold of my hand and lowered the two of us to the concrete.

'Nice piece of detective work,' I said. 'How did you find us?'

The major rose athletically and strode to the centre of the room. 'You know?' he said. 'I've never liked women who talk too much. Shut her up?'

Out of the corner of my eye I saw the white shirt behind me raise his weapon and bring it down to pistol whip the back of my head. Arny reached out and caught the full force of the blow on the back of his hand. There was a crunch as if one or two small bones had been broken but my little brother kept his arm aloft to catch a second blow.

'Oh, lovely,' said the general. 'Family unity. We have our first hero'.

The white shirt caught Arny another blow, this one across the ear. It should have knocked him out but he merely glared back at the young policeman, blood dribbling down his neck. I was terribly proud of him but I feared he'd not be able to take another blow. It was obvious why Ketthai and his henchmen were there. It was a termination. Unless I could think of something in a hurry, none of us would be leaving Khin's house alive. The only good news was the fact we weren't blown away as soon as we entered. That meant there was something the invaders needed. This would buy us some time.

The major walked to Sissy who was still on his knees, still grinning like a fool.

'Where's the Burmese?' Ketthai asked.

Of course, that was the loose end. They had to get rid of all of us.

'Probably a lot of them in Yangon,' Sissy smiled.

It was the wrong time to be trying out new material. The major kicked out at Sissy who was able to sway backwards slightly and avoid the full impact of the boot. But he continued to push his luck.

'You do know in Thai culture a gentleman takes off his shoes before entering a house?'

'Sissy, shut up,' I yelled in English but too late to stop him getting a painful toe poke in the ribs followed by a thump on the head from the butt of the rifle. He fell to the floor, still smiling. The back of his head was slick with blood that glistened in the light from the back door.

The major nodded for two of his men to put down their weapons. They grabbed me by the arms and hoisted me to my feet. In my mind, the odds had just improved. Only one man with a gun trained on us now, almost an even fight. If only Arny and Sissy had been proficient in the martial arts. Body building and fashion modelling didn't prepare a man for a moment like this. The major turned his attention to me.

'You never stop being a pain in my backside, girl,' he said. 'Do you know how much you've cost me over time? How many years' work you wasted for me with your nosing around?'

I thought he was talking about the movie but he seemed to be focused on something else.

'Do I know you?' I asked.

'Yeah, you know me. But you'll know me a lot better when I've finished with you today.'

'Did I write something?'

He took hold of my hair roughly and reached into his back pocket. The switchblade was twenty centimetres long and flipped open with ease. It changed the format of our demise in my mind. There would be no gunshots. Three throats cut in silence, no alarm. If there was to be a move from us it had to be soon.

'Remind me,' I said. 'I'd hate to have my throat cut without knowing why.'

'Some gambling joints within three blocks of a police station,' he said. 'Remember that? It wasn't well written but it was enough to get the national press involved. Enough to have my operation shut down.'

I remembered. But I'd written it under a pseudonym and I hadn't known who the kingpin was. I didn't have a name. He got away with it.'

'You broke the law,' I said. 'You deserved to get busted.'

'The law's there to be broken,' Ketthai said.

'You should have been jailed. I bet all they did was transfer you.'

'Yes. To fucking Fang – the asshole of the universe. Don't think I haven't been waiting for the chance to thank you for that.'

'And look at you. Six years later and you're still killing and breaking all the laws you swore to uphold.'

'And you couldn't resist the temptation to come up and take me on again, could you?'

He'd got it in his paranoid mind that this was some sort of vendetta on my part.

'I had no idea who you were,' I said.

'Liar. You thought you'd just walk in and do your spying and nobody would notice?' he said. 'You're hopeless. One of my boys made you that night you went to see the director. He remembered you from Chiang Mai. You didn't even have the sense to put on glasses and a false wig.'

He looked up at his men who were obliged to laugh at his joke. It wasn't the wisest move to antagonize a homicidal police major holding a switchblade but I needed time.

'I'm hopeless?' I said. 'How many times did you try to kill us or set us up? Talk about incompetent.'

The major was calm again. He knew it would soon be over. For his own amusement he began to hack off my hair close to the scalp with his blade. I was very touchy about my hair.

'I delegated,' he said. 'And when you delegate you send the best men you've got. And from a place like Fang the best wouldn't get a job peddling a tricycle taxi in Bangkok. That's why I came in person today. To get the job done right.'

'Hear that, guys?' I said casually. 'Your boss thinks you haven't got the brains to drive a *samlor*. Bet that makes you feel good.'

I got a knee in my side for the effort.

'Delegating someone to kill for you still counts as murder in this country,' I said. 'It's called solicitation. That makes you accountable for the deaths. Are you going to kill me too?'

'Yes,' he said. 'But not until after we've defiled you. Look, let's make this easier. All I need to know is where the Burmese went. Then we can wrap things up neatly and all go home.'

He shifted his attention to our weakest link. For Arny's benefit he mimed the sweep of his blade across my throat. He laughed and glared at my brother.

'You don't want me to cut your sister's head off, do you now?' the major asked.

'No,' said Arny.

'Then all you have to do is tell me where the Burmese is.'

'Here,' came a voice.

From that moment we could really have done with a slow motion camera to appreciate the events that took place and the speed at which they occurred. Khin appeared at the back door with a brick in either hand. In a remarkably well coordinated effort she smashed them onto the heads of the two men holding me and they dropped to their knees. Sissy and I crashed into the major at about the same time causing him to fall against the wall and drop the blade. Arny kicked the armed white shirt in the balls. He doubled over and lowered his weapon. This gave Khin time to dig two fingers into his eye sockets and take the gun. By the time the cops had gathered themselves they already had weapons trained on them and were having their hands tied with site marking string. To put down any idea of a resurrection, Khin released the safety and fired a round into the wall above the policemen's heads. Masonry rained down on them. By then Sissy was already using her phone to call the CCC.

When the military unit arrived at the house in Wieng Kum Kam they found four men tied with string and three new bruises on the ribs of Major Khettai. A lot has been said to the detriment of gratuitous violence. There are arguments that the hardest but most satisfying reaction to abuse is to forgive. But whoever wrote that obviously hadn't been held up at gunpoint and terrorized. Defile me, would you? There is something healing about landing a good kick at the torso of a bully and all of us but Khin had allowed ourselves that unforgiving luxury while we waited for backup.

Once the police had been carted off, the amok runners sat on the garden wall watching the smudgy sun set beyond the river. The birds went into a frenzy as if they'd just noticed the day was coming to an end and there were a hundred things still to do.

'All right,' Sissy said, 'I've got one question.'

'Only one?' I said.

'How did they know we were here in Wieng Kum Kam?'

'Maybe the taxi driver spotted us and did his civic duty by phoning it in,' I said. 'Wouldn't be surprised if the major put out a reward.'

'Maybe they put a magnet tracer on the Suzuki,' said Arny.

'When?' Sissy asked.

'Probably the day we showed 'em how smart we were by driving to Fang police headquarters with the press,' I said.

'I thought Thai police were technologically challenged.'

'They watch TV,' I reminded him. 'That's probably how they found us when we drove up to the temple that evening too.'

'They didn't find "us", Jimm,' said Sissy. 'It was Miss Super Investigative Journalist they were after. Nobody wanted to kill me. I was an innocent bystander.'

'Yeah,' I agreed. 'Sorry about that.'

We moved to the Suzuki seats. We were still numb from events so we couldn't feel the mosquitoes.

'I think we were pretty exceptional,' I said.

'Khin was the star,' said Sissy, switching to English.

'I'm going to embroider her a belt,' I said.

Khin had been on another planet since the ambush, floating in her own thoughts.

'Khin!' I shouted.

'Yes?'

'I'm going to embroider you a belt.'

'Saying?'

'Two at one blow.'

'I'd rather not get a reputation for knocking down policemen,' she said.

'Why not? The legend would spread out of control and the Burmese junta would tremble in their boots at the very sound of your name. You'd be the masked avenger with no respect for uniforms.'

'As with most impetuous acts, the results were greater than the sum of the thought that went into them,' she said. 'I merely brought back the brick samples to compare them with the images in my text book. I hadn't planned to lay low thugs with them. But I must say you have something of a gift for violence yourself.'

'Mair raised me a tomboy. There was a mix-up at home. I got the male genes and Sissy got all my female ones. Plus I have a sort of pet hate about men poking guns into the back of my head. Why did you come back so soon, by the way?'

'Back to the house?'

'Yes. You told us you'd be staying down at the river till it got dark.'

'I simultaneously had a revelation and a recollection,' she said. 'I needed to check my notes. There was something from the reign of King Khoi of the seventeenth century. The mention of a beacon mid-river that marked the boundary of Wieng Kum Kam. May I invite you to join me in a little research?'

'Lead the way, my guru.'

After her heroic deeds I'd developed an even keener respect for her and was prepared to indulge her in the treasure fantasy for one more day. I followed her inside to the living room where two large cardboard boxes had been overturned in the melee. Paperwork was sprawled across the floor.

'You think the bricks we found might have come from the beacon?' I asked.

'Nobody seems certain as to what year the river actually changed its course. As there are no rocks or rapids on this stretch of the river it had always seemed odd to me that there was any need for a beacon at all.'

'Ah, so you're hypothesizing that it wasn't a beacon at all but the remains of a stupa that accidentally found itself in the middle of the new Ping,' I said.

'You have a natural bent for this work, my dear. You should give up the folly of being a reporter and come to be my personal assistant.'

'That's really tempting.'

'It is merely a theory of course but it would explain why the experts had found no trace of it. Ah, here it is.'

She produced a green file labelled 'Burmese King Thado Khoi, 1607 to 1608. After a little thumbing she found what she was looking for.

'Here,' she said, and began to read from the file. 'The light on the spired beacon at Wieng Kum Kam was the signal for King Khoi and his nobles to stop for the night.'

'Hmm. A spire on a beacon?'

'Doesn't it sound a bit like a stupa, to you?' she asked.

'Within my limited realm of expertise on beacons, it does suggest the beacon wasn't lit up to stop boats getting stuck on sandbanks but rather to stop people hitting the beacon. Which in turn suggests it wasn't a beacon.'

'Exactly.'

'So, what do you think? I asked. 'It was about to fall down anyway from the pressure of the current, and they took it apart?'

'Perhaps intending to rebuild it.'

'Do you suppose they went down as far as the foundations?'

'It would have been exceedingly difficult to excavate under water given the lack of equipment, and it's unlikely the rumour of Mangrai's treasure had passed down through the subsequent three hundred years. My guess is they'd give up on the base and build new foundations elsewhere. But due to wars and other distractions, the rebuilding was put off.'

'So if this was really the Pa Tan temple, the original foundations would still be there at the bottom of the river.'

'It is a tantalizing prospect don't you think?'

'So, let's go dig,' I said.

'I'm afraid after all those years the base of the stupa could be considerably deep. It would have sunk over time and been covered in numerous layers of silt.'

'So, what do we need?'

'Nothing short of a dredger,' she said.

'So let's get one.'

Khin laughed. 'That would be extortionately expensive.'

'Give me a ball-park figure.'

'Ooh, I don't know. It could cost anything up to six thousand baht per day. That's almost two-hundred dollars American.'

I smiled.

'You do realize we just saved a movie company several million dollars in overrun costs?'

Chapter 34

"You're gonna need a bigger boat."
Jaws (1975)

Arny had expressed the opinion that dredgers weren't likely to be just sitting around waiting to be hired but he was wrong. At the Ao Daeng yard just twelve kilometres downstream from Wieng Kum Kam there were three rust-pitted dredgers moored idle. They'd worked on the weir at Pa Sang then found themselves stranded by it. They came complete with pilots desperate for work. Given the annual floods, the Chiang Mai authorities had no objections to dredging but lacked the funds to pay for it themselves. I was even able to talk the yard owner down to a daily fee of five-thousand baht including fuel and labour.

While Sissy drove the jeep back to Khin's house, Arny and I travelled upstream on the clunky metal raft. The craft appeared to defy any of the basic rules of aqua-dynamics. There was no recognizable bow or stern. It was a top-heavy basting tray with so much equipment on the deck it was unthinkable that it could float at all. Yet it sat high in the water and seemed to skim over the shallows. Two enormous gear-wheels drove a conveyor loaded with metal scoops. These dug deeper and deeper into the river bottom and carried the mud up to a large hopper. It was a simple design which, Khin informed everyone, hadn't changed much in the past hundred years.

Neither the boat pilot nor the yard owner had shown any interest in Khin's qualifications to be conducting the dig. The skipper hadn't even asked the purpose of the mission. When we arrived at a point parallel to the previous day's brick heap he was told just to chug up and down in a grid pattern and make shallow inroads until they hit something.

For lunch Sissy brought two cartons of Singha Beer and six pizzas. From there on the afternoon merged into a boozy sing-along boat cruise that didn't go anywhere.

'You know, this isn't half bad,' Sissy decided. 'With a bit of luck we might even get in one more day of boating before our dredger contract's up.'

Khin hadn't once deserted her post at the hopper. She did accept a bottle of beer but she was up to her shoulders in mud most of the time so didn't get around to drinking any. She dove into the slushy river slime with the enthusiasm of a grade-schooler at a sandpit. She squeezed out pebbles and rocks and washed them in a bucket of water and discarded them. She spoke to herself constantly in Burmese. She was a woman with a mission. We made several attempts to help but she turned us away. I really felt sorry for her that afternoon. She'd researched so long and tried so hard and every attempt at finding the treasure had hit a wall. I knew she'd never find her prize and I got the feeling she knew it too. Perhaps it was the chase that invigorated her.

We'd emptied ten skips of mud onto the far bank and probably created foundations for a four million baht riverside property above the marshes. But nothing that passed Khin's gaze inspired her.

'What exactly are we looking for, Khin?' Arny asked once, looking over her shoulder into the big tub of mud.

'Residue of masonry,' she said. 'Somewhat similar to the bricks we encountered yesterday but flatter and thicker. If the foundation is indeed here it would begin with a layer of bricks three feet deep.'

'And then?'

'Beneath that is a mystery.'

'Mystery's your middle name,' I shouted. 'Khin Mystery Thein Aye.'

'Yes,' she replied. 'But in this particular scenario, the mystery exists because of the personality of the plaster. As I have told you repeatedly, any valuables buried under a stupa would have been encased in some form of plaster or heavy-density clay. In a land-based stupa, gold Buddha images from the twelfth and thirteenth century have been uncovered still embedded in their original plaster cast. But the stupa of the Pa Tan temple would have been under water for centuries. If the casing was plaster, it isn't inconceivable it dissolved and has been washed away. This would expose the metal artefacts to the ravages of rusting.'

'So, why don't you just dredge deeper and get through the bricks sooner?' I asked.

'Jimm, Jimm, Jimm! Impatience killed off the tiger. It's impossible to estimate just how far down we need to go. A conveyor running too deep could cause irreparable damage to a structure or to anything it contained.'

'Khin.'

'Yes, Jimm?'

'Promise me you won't get disappointed.'

'About?'

'If this comes to nothing.'

'Oh, ye of little faith.'

'We won't think any less of you if you don't find anything. In fact, I doubt we could think much less of you.'

'You're too kind.'

The remaining Singha beers were in a net being dragged behind the dredger in the water. This didn't exactly chill them but it did leave them at what the British liked to call 'room temperature'. Rooms can get pretty cold in the UK so it was certainly cool enough for us. It went down well with dried river prawns and peanuts and the time kicked along nicely filled with funny conversation, a swim now and then, and awful singing. The boat was booked until six-thirty and all the next day from eight.

The sun was low enough to peer beneath the smog and make silvery fingerprints on the surface of the water. We had half an hour left on our day's contract, paid for generously by our movie director, when we heard an ominous metallic crunch from below. The dredger groaned as if it had come upon an old deserted truck fuselage on the river bed. The craft lurched and listed to one side before the motor settled back into its old bronchial rhythm.

'Was that me?' Sissy asked.

'No, it was the boat,' Arny reassured him.

'We walked to the amidships where we found Khin leaning over the railing getting her bearings.

'Quick,' she shouted. 'Get a fix. Find yourself a landmark on either flank and commit it to memory.'

'What's up, Khin?' Arny asked.

'Look,' she smiled and turned back to the trough of mud. 'Look what that little prang just now has conjured up.'

She plunged her hand into the gunk and emerged with a small nugget of red brick. 'We have our foundation.'

Arny hopped with delight. 'Khin, are you certain?'

'As certain as I shall ever be.'

My older brother and I exchanged familiar raised eyebrows. Khin was crying wolf again and our little brother had come to gather up the sheep. But he'd learn. He'd learn.

Chapter 35

"Back where I come from there are men who do nothing all day but good deeds. They are called phila ... er, phila ... er, yes, er, Good Deed Doers."
The Wizard of Oz (1939)

It was May. The rains had arrived on schedule and cleaned up the skies. They'd washed the slopes of the mountain, and brightened the murky moods. The symphony of night-time coughing from dusty lungs had been replaced by the burping of toads. From the deck on Doi Suthep you could see all the way to the mountains of Phayao and beyond. Chiang Mai had become crisp and focused.

Bunny Savage was in Italy filming a love story in Lago D'Orta with Harrison Ford. It would have been an icky, dirty old man – pretty young girl movie if he'd been anyone but Harrison Ford. But the projections suggested the world was in desperate need of love on the big screen and Ford fancied a month in Italy so he was being offered at a discount.

Siam was into post-production and scheduled for a Christmas – New Year release. OB had moved onto his next project – another remake of Fellini's Roma with De Caprio playing the role of the young Fellini, and San Francisco playing the role of Rome. All the Fellini adoration had probably clouded the fact that Roma was a crap movie to begin with but OB had reached the top step of the pedestal. It gave him a view of the universe and the balls to do whatever he liked. Stuff profits.

Under pressure from the US embassy, the junta had expedited the corruption trial of Ketthai and his cohorts and my brothers and I had been star witnesses for the prosecution. The trials in Bangkok had gone unreported in the national press. Much the same as suicide bombings in Iraq leaving fewer than twenty victims no longer warranted a mention, serious corruption stories in Thailand in May had to start at around a billion baht to deserve a headline. There was a lot of competition. The major was in the minors – unworthy of an editorial. His name vanished from the records at the same time as he disappeared from life on earth. Military run courts had a pragmatic approach to justice.

And then there was that joke. A fat girl, a bodybuilder, a transsexual and a Burmese were sitting on a deck overlooking the shimmering night lights of Chiang Mai. The transsexual turned to the fat girl and said, 'I'm gone, man.'

'Where have you gone?' I asked.

'Ooh, heaven?' said Sissy. 'I don't know. This is some serious weed, sister. Where's it from?'

'Laos.'

'And doesn't that just explain why the Lao are so laid back. How's Khin taking it?'

I looked to my right, past a snoring Arny to a comatose Burmese.

'She was unconscious as soon as we took it out the plastic bag,' I said.

'She still breathing?'

'There's a slight movement under her shirt,' I said. 'It could be maggots.'

'No,' said Sissy. 'Khin'll never die. She's a goddess.'

'Well, she sure has got herself a condominium and a pile of gold up in heaven,' I agreed. 'More than she's ever going to see down here with us mortals.'

'You aren't still sore at her?'

'You kidding? After all that work we put in to finding her treasure for her?'

'What did you expect her to do?'

'I don't know. Share it with us?'

'Now, that's not Khin, and you know it.'

'Least she could have done was slip us a ruby each as a thank you. When she was documenting the stuff she had lots of chances to slide a ceremonial dagger down her underwear. We could be home-owners – retired – comfortable for the rest of our days. But no. What does she do? Calls the Department of Fine Arts and a dozen witnesses. And what did that get her?'

'Kudos. Credit.'

'Not the kind of credit you can spend,' I said. 'She's back tutoring and relying on us to keep her alive just like the good old days. Meanwhile, a billion *baht*'s worth of treasure sits down there in a safe in some Bangkok museum. What do you bet it'll be on some rich collector's shelf before the year's out?'

'I wouldn't know about that but I'd bet Chiang Mai University finds some way to get her legal and put her on faculty so they can lay claim to the discovery. They've already asked her when she'd be available.'

'Well, *there*'s a prize. A job at CMU.'

'It's what she wants.'

'She's nuts.'

'Yeah. But you've got to love her.'

'Yeah. I know.'

We each took the final puff that would drop us over the edge. We'd made a few resolutions that evening. We promised to ease up on the weed. I promised I'd start referring to Sissy as 'she' to avoid further misunderstandings. Sissy decided to work full time on computer scams and say goodbye to acting. And we crooked our little fingers together in a promise that before the turn of the century we would be writing and producing multi-million dollar movies directed by our beloved Clint. We found the strength to slur a few final words before we dropped off.

A fat girl, a bodybuilder, a transsexual and a Burmese were sitting on a deck snoring with surprising harmony on the skirt of Doi Suthep. They dreamed, not of better things, because things could not be better, but rather of the things they had. Too few people appreciated the bird that fluttered in the hand.

CPSIA information can be obtained at www.ICGtesting.com
Printed in the USA
LVOW10s2129100816

499907LV00013B/109/P